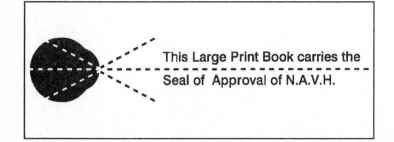

This Large Print Book carries the
Seal of Approval of N.A.V.H.

A SNOW COUNTRY
CHRISTMAS

A SNOW COUNTRY CHRISTMAS

LINDA LAEL MILLER

WHEELER PUBLISHING
A part of Gale, a Cengage Company

Farmington Hills, Mich • San Francisco • New York • Waterville, Maine
Meriden, Conn • Mason, Ohio • Chicago

Copyright © 2017 by Hometown Girl Makes Good, Inc.
Wheeler Publishing, a part of Gale, a Cengage Company.

Wheeler Publishing Large Print Hardcover.
The text of this Large Print edition is unabridged.
Other aspects of the book may vary from the original edition.
Set in 16 pt. Plantin.

**LIBRARY OF CONGRESS CIP DATA ON FILE.
CATALOGUING IN PUBLICATION FOR THIS BOOK
IS AVAILABLE FROM THE LIBRARY OF CONGRESS.**

ISBN-13: 978-1-4328-4399-1 (hardcover)
ISBN-10: 1-4328-4399-0 (hardcover)

Published in 2017 by arrangement with Harlequin Books S.A.

Printed in the United States of America
1 2 3 4 5 6 7 21 20 19 18 17

A SNOW COUNTRY CHRISTMAS

December 23rd
The young lady sat with her chin on fist, the firelight shining off her dark hair. She was reflective but not pensive, content in her solitude on this cold evening. A log in the old stone fireplace snapped and crackled and there was the smell of pine in the air. Her father's old dog lay asleep at her feet, gently snoring; the sound comforting. Two days to Christmas and she'd spend it alone for the first time.

From the opening paragraph of
The Aspen Trail
Matthew Brighton, 1965

1

Raine McCall first frowned at the screen and then stared at the clock.

Her computer was right. Two in the morning? No way.

Oh, she'd be the first to admit that when she was working she lost track of time, but she was always there to put her daughter on the school bus and make sure Daisy had done her homework and had a healthy breakfast.

She'd always suffered from what she called WSS. Whimsical Sleep Schedule.

Awake at all hours, losing track of time if the muse was in the mood, and she'd been guilty of falling asleep in the chair at her desk. Daisy had told her more than once, with a maturity beyond her years, she thought she worked too hard, but then Raine didn't really think of it as work. Spinning dream images into reality was a unique joy and she felt sorry for every person in the world that had a job they disliked.

She wasn't the only one awake, either. Taking a break, she checked her email and was startled. Mick Branson? *The* Mick Branson had sent her a message? Hotshot Hollywood executive, way too focused, and no sense of humor — though come to think of it, he did smile now and then. He was good-looking, but she couldn't get beyond the sophisticated polish. She was a Wyoming girl through and through and thousand dollar suits weren't her preference. Give her a hat, jeans, and some worn boots.

Of course she'd met the man quite a few times at the ranch because he was the driving force behind the documentaries that Slater Carson, her ex-boyfriend and the father of her child, made, but getting an email from him was a definite first. Sent five minutes ago? She was too intrigued not to open it.

> I'm going to be in Mustang Creek for the holidays. Can we have a business meeting? Maybe over dinner?

That *was* interesting, but currently she was up to her ears in deadlines trying to produce artwork for the labels for Mountain Vineyards wines. Her graphic design business had really taken off, and she wasn't sure she could handle another project.

From what she knew of Mick Branson, it wouldn't be a small one, either.

She typed back. When did you have in mind?

Tomorrow night? If you don't already have plans, that is.

On Christmas Eve?

Well, Daisy did usually spend that evening with her father's family and Raine spent it alone with a nice glass of wine and a movie. They always invited her, but she went the next day instead for the big dinner celebration and skipped the night before in favor of solitude. It was never that they made her feel like an outsider; quite the opposite, but Slater needed some time with his daughter to make memories without Raine always in the background. So while she appreciated the invitation, she'd always declined. It had been difficult when Daisy was little to spend such a magical evening away from her, but he was entitled. He was a wonderful father.

She typed: On the 24th of December, I assure you no place is open in Mustang Creek. This isn't California. You'd have to come to my place and I usually just eat a hamburger

11

and drink wine.

He wrote back: That sounds fine. I like burgers and I enjoy wine. Let me bring the beverages. Please excuse me if I'm inviting myself.

She couldn't decide if he had, or if she'd done it. She really did need to get more sleep now and then. She typed: Mountain Vineyards for the wine.

You got it.

Have a safe flight.

Thank you, but I'm already here. See you tomorrow. Don't mention to anyone, especially Slater, that I'm in town please.

Raine sat back and let out a breath. She hadn't ever anticipated spending an evening with someone like Mick Branson, much less Christmas Eve.

Luckily, she thought, she'd thoroughly cleaned the house the day before when she realized that sound she abstractly heard in the background was the vacuum. Daisy was *voluntarily* doing a chore she usually argued over? Raine decided then and there — once she recovered from her shock — that maybe she had been spending too much time in her office. Sure enough, the house needed dusting, the kitchen floor had crumbs on it and the laundry room was in dire need of a workout.

Not that someone like Mr. Hollywood Executive Mick Branson, who probably lived in a mansion in Beverly Hills, would be impressed with her small and eclectic house anyway, no matter how tidy. Wait until he got a look at her Christmas tree. There was no theme to the ornaments; if something caught her eye, she bought and put it up. There were owls, glittery reindeer, a glass shrimp with wings wearing a boa, all right alongside her grandmother's collection of English traditional antique glass orbs in brilliant colors. Those heirlooms were hung up high thanks to Mr. Bojangles, her enormous Maine coon cat. He was somewhat of a reclusive character, but he became positively playful when the Christmas tree went up. Walking past it usually meant an unexpected guerilla attack on your ankles because he considered it his covert hiding place every December. Therefore the ornaments on the bottom were soft stuffed squirrels and bunnies with a few fake pine cones he could bat around. Add in Daisy's giant dog, Samson, who accidentally knocked an ornament off every time he walked by, and her tree had no hope.

"Definitely not a designer tree, unless a deranged leprechaun arranged it" was how Daisy described it.

Raine loved it.

It was exactly her style. There was nothing wrong with being quirky. She went and switched off the lights and headed off to bed, wondering how she'd gotten roped into this situation.

Hollywood Hotshot Mick Branson eating hamburgers at her house on Christmas Eve?

Slater Carson was going to laugh himself into a fit.

The plane had touched down on a snowy runway and Mick had said a small prayer of thanks for an experienced pilot and maybe some luck of the season as the snow continued to pile up. It had been a bumpy ride and he wasn't at all a nervous flyer, but coming over the mountains he'd had a moment or two.

He'd been everywhere. Asia, Africa, South America, Australia, Europe . . . he lived in Los Angeles, but he liked Wyoming. It felt like being on vacation and he could really, really use a vacation.

It wouldn't be a hardship to see Raine McCall again, either.

The thought surprised him because she was *so* not his type. Frothy skirts, and as far as he could tell she thought makeup was optional, or maybe forgot it altogether, and if she owned a pair of heels he'd be surprised. Her artistic temperament was the antithesis of his rigidly corporate lifestyle, but he somehow found it intriguing. She was naturally beautiful without trying. Maybe that was it. There was no artifice to Raine — what you saw was what you got. Not to mention he had a feeling she could care less how much money he made. Material things, he guessed, to her, were little more than a necessity now and then.

Anyway, he had planned this trip with a dual purpose.

He wanted to surprise Slater, who was not just a colleague but a friend, with the television premier of the documentary of *Wild West . . . Still Wild* — and he wanted to see Raine. Two separate goals but also intertwined, since Slater and Raine had a past and shared a daughter. Slater was now happily married to someone else, but through a few very casual questions, Mick knew Raine wasn't seeing anyone.

This might get complicated and he hated complications. Business deals were a dance back and forth but he kept his personal life as simple as possible.

Raine was far from simple. Her art was exemplary and over the top, and the vivid mermaid label she'd created for the Carson winery's sparkling wine had resulted in more bottles sold in one day upon release than were sold of all their other wines combined, and they had been doing quite well before. Somehow he doubted Raine even registered the triumph.

But he wasn't interested in her for her talent — well, he was impressed, but that wasn't first and foremost in his mind. Maybe opposites did attract, though if you'd told him that before he'd met her through the Carson family, he'd have laughed it off.

He wasn't laughing now. It wasn't that he didn't have a good reason to be in Wyoming at the moment anyway, but he was essentially there because of a certain woman he couldn't seem to get off his mind.

Grace Carson met him in the dining room of the Bliss River Resort and Spa, her eyes sparkling, and gave him a welcoming hug. Slater really did have good taste in women because his wife was a stunning redhead with a confident air. She also apparently had a good memory, because almost immediately a waiter came over with coffee and a rack of rye toast, which was his favorite.

She joined him, pouring coffee for them both. "Do you have any idea how hard it is to not tell Slater about Christmas Day?"

"I've actually struggled with it myself, so maybe I do." He admired the view of the snow-capped mountains out the huge windows as he sipped his coffee and thought about all the strings he'd pulled. Considerable was the answer. He looked back at Grace, which was also a pleasure. "The time slot was the hardest part. But everyone is pretty much home, and hopefully by then Christmas dinner will be over and there will be a worldwide desire to watch something other than the old classics."

She added cream to her coffee. "I think it's a brilliant idea. You do realize you just usurped my gift to him, which was a new saddle. He'll probably kiss *you* under the mistletoe instead of me."

Mick chuckled. "I doubt it, but if it happens, let's not catch that on film." Not knowing remote cameras were taking footage, Slater's younger brother Drake had gotten caught in a romantic moment with his now wife, Luce, and was none too happy about it being used in the film, but had grudgingly signed the release.

"Maybe Raine will kiss you instead." Grace took a sip from her silver-rimmed cup, a knowing look in her eyes.

He'd never understood how women had magical powers when it came to sensing a possible romance. Men just blundered on, unaware, and females were like wolves sniffing the air. He was a man who played angles, so he admitted noncommittally, "I can't imagine any man minding that. How is the resort business these days?"

She caught on to that just as easily. "Subject changed. I can take a hint. It's going well. Ski season is in full swing. We're packed. The spa is booked out two months. The owner is pleased and it keeps me busy and, well, I'm expecting again. Luce is also in baby mode. We're just waiting for the same kind of announcement from Mace and Kelly. Then all the cousins can grow up together."

Mick pictured a bunch of toddlers running wild around the sprawling Carson ranch. To his surprise, the image was immensely appealing. He hadn't had much exposure to babies; his only brother was childless by choice even though he'd been married a long time. He and his wife tended to spend the winter in France or at their house in the Caribbean, and as an investment banker, Ran could work from any-where, so their attitude reflected their sophisticated lifestyle.

Prior to his business association with Slater, he hadn't thought about it much, but Mick had to acknowledge that his upbringing had left a hole in his life. Warm family gatherings had just never happened. His parents traveled widely when his father was alive and now it was tradition to meet his mother at the country club for Christmas dinner.

Elegant, but not exactly cozy. He'd been to celebrations at the Carson ranch before and they were usually quite the boisterous experience. He said, "Congratulations. Slater is a lucky man all the way around."

"He'll certainly be one tomorrow," Grace replied with a smile. "I haven't said a word to anyone — although Blythe knows, which means Harry knows."

"Raine knows I'm in town." He gave what he hoped was a casual shrug. "We have a business meeting tonight and she said no restaurants would be open, so she invited me over."

Arched brows rose higher. "Did she now? She's breaking her burger and glass of wine tradition?"

"No. I was informed that's the menu."

Grace gave a laugh of real merriment. "Only Raine would serve Mick Branson a burger. I love Raine but she is on the eclectic side. That's why I was surprised the two of you hit it off so well. She's right about Christmas Eve, by the way — we even close the restaurants here at the resort and the spa. Guests can pre-order special bags with gourmet sandwiches and salads that will be delivered via room service, but quite frankly, I just don't believe in making anyone work who would rather be with their family on Christmas. A few staff members would rather work for holiday pay, so the resort is open, but not the dining choices. In town everything is closed."

Vaguely he registered her words about the holiday, but his mind was caught on what she'd said about Raine. *Hit it off?* He chose not to comment. He could negotiate deals involving millions of dollars, but personal discussions were not his strong suit. "Los Angeles is a little different."

"Oh, I bet." Grace was definitely amused. Her phone beeped and she rose. "Excuse me, but that sound means something needs my attention. I'll see you tomorrow."

After she left he finished his toast and coffee, checked his email via his phone, and headed out to his rental car. It was lightly snowing and briskly cold, the car dusted over in white, and he wished he'd thought about bringing some gloves. It wasn't something that occurred to him back in L.A. when he packed for the trip.

The wine shop was on the main street and someone had done an artistic job of decorating the windows with snowflakes. The bells on the huge wreath on the door jingled as Mick walked in. There were several other customers and he noted Kelly Carson, Slater's sister-in-law, was the one sitting behind the old polished counter. She looked cute wearing an elf hat and a surprised expression.

Good, his lucky day.

Or so he hoped, but it was yet another person to swear to secrecy. Her eyes had widened as she recognized him.

There was just no such thing as a secret in Mustang Creek. He'd heard that the last time he'd been in town and really hadn't believed it, but was now starting to feel like living proof.

"Merry Christmas, Mick," Kelly called as he approached.

"Merry Christmas," he said. "Let me make an educated guess and assume you're working because you wouldn't ask any of the employees to so they could be with their

21

families."

She nodded and the fuzzy tassel on her hat bobbed. "You're right. Absolutely. We're only open until noon today anyway, holiday hours . . . I guess I didn't realize you were in town. No one mentioned it."

"No one knows." Well, not true. Grace, Blythe, Harry and Raine knew, and now Kelly. He smiled wryly. "Let me rephrase. I'd prefer if Slater didn't find out I'm here. It's about both business and friendship, so if you can keep it to yourself until tomorrow, I'd appreciate it."

She sent him a wink. "My lips are sealed."

"I knew I could count on you. Now, tell me, best wine to go with a burger would be . . . what?"

"I hate to disappoint you, but Bad Billy's won't be open."

The biker bar was legendary for its burgers. "I'm not actually getting my burger from Billy's."

She blinked. "Oh . . . oh! Raine?"

It was tempting to deny it, but . . . well, why bother? Clearly her Christmas Eve burgers tradition was well-known. "We have a business meeting tonight. What kind of wine does she usually buy?"

"The Wildfire Merlot." Kelly said it promptly, her expression alight with humor.

"She also likes Soaring Eagle Chardonnay. Either one would be fine. At the end of the day, Mace always tells me to drink a wine you like with food you like. Don't worry about the rest of it. He thinks snobbish pairing is overrated."

"People all over California just fainted dead away because you said that."

"People all over California buy our wines," she countered with a mischievous elfin grin that matched her festive hat. "So he seems to know what he's doing."

Tough to argue with that. "I'll take a few bottles of each, plus some for the Christmas gathering tomorrow, including the new sparkling wine. Just give me a case."

2

It wasn't like she didn't consider what she wore, but on a scale of one to ten she would rate herself maybe a five when it came to how much thought and time she usually put into her attire.

Tonight for some reason, Raine was on the higher end of the scale.

The long red skirt and clingy black blouse looked nice, but were not exactly hamburger-worthy, she decided with a critical eye before she changed into jeans and a teal blue silk sweater. Except it occurred to her that if she dribbled ketchup or spilled even a drop of wine the sweater would be toast and she'd have to toss it — she'd known at the time it was an impractical purchase but had loved it too much not to buy it — so she changed for a third time. Black leggings and a patterned gray sweater dress won the day, comfortable but certainly dressier than she'd usually choose for a night home alone.

Well, she wasn't going to be alone. She even set the table — which would never have happened on her traditional Christmas Eve — with what she called her December plates, white with tiny candy canes on them. Daisy had seen them when they'd been out shopping when she was six years old and begged, so Raine caved and bought them. Every year when the plates came out, it signaled the holiday season for her daughter and the sentimental value was priceless. Even though she'd been a classic example of a starving artist and had been trying to launch her business at the time, she'd also bought a set of silverware whose handles were etched with reindeer and a sleigh.

It was ironic in a good way to think someone as successful as Mick Branson wanted to meet with her on a professional level and would eat off the dishes that she'd bought when she really couldn't afford them. Now she was so busy she doubted she could accept whatever it was he wanted to discuss even if she was interested.

Mr. Bojangles wandered past with a feline yawn, headed for his food bowl, but stopping to be petted. It was like a royal decree when a cat of his size demanded to be scratched behind the ears. Raine stroked his head. "What do you think of the table? Fancy enough for a hotshot executive?"

He yawned again, his gold-green eyes reflecting doubt. She said defensively, "Hey, I paid twenty bucks for those dishes."

His furry face expressed his skepticism that the plates were worth even that. She argued his point. "Daisy loves them."

He didn't disagree, just headed off to the kitchen to chomp loudly out of his bowl. His ample backside was normal for his breed, but his love of food didn't help matters. His vet, Jax Locke, had been diplomatic in suggesting she could maybe curtail the cat treats.

Raine agreed, but Jangles — as she called him face-to-face — was a contender when it came to getting his way. There was not much in the way of compromise on his part.

The snow was beginning to blow a little and she had started a fire in her fireplace with the push of a button. She liked ambiance and watching the flames, but as a single female didn't want to haul in logs, so she'd had a gas insert put in a few years ago. Bypassing Christmas music, she put on some soft classical in the background, and without the World's Largest Puppy — Samson — tearing around, the house felt downright serene. Daisy always took him with her to the ranch and he loved running free with the other dogs. The backyard at Raine's just wasn't as exciting as herding cattle with Drake and the other hands. Maybe when he got a little older Samson would be content to just bask in the sun. As it stood, he wanted to run amok.

Red, the head ranch hand, called the dog a log-legged galoot. That seemed about right.

When Raine saw the arc of headlights in the big front window and glanced at the fairy tale clock on the mantel, Cinderella's glass slipper was pointed right at six sharp. Mick Branson was right on time.

She, on the other hand, was perpetually late to everything. Maybe being awake at two in the morning was the only thing they had in common. She opened the door before he knocked and in return got a capricious swirl of snow blowing into the tiny foyer.

"Thanks," he said as he came in. "The wind is really picking up. A Merry Christmas with all the appropriate special effects." He studied her as he wiped his boots on the mat inside the door. "It's nice to see you again."

"And you as well." She shut the door, peering through the side panel of glass. "It is coming down out there, isn't it? So pretty."

"From safe in here, it's very pretty," he said with his all too fleeting smile. "The wine is in this bag, and where do you want my coat?"

She recognized the bag because she'd designed the print on it. The M for Mountain Vineyards was flanked by pine trees and a hawk sat on a branch on one side. "I'll take your coat, and the kitchen is through that doorway right there. It's impossible to get lost in this house."

"It's charming." He glanced around as he slipped off his wool coat.

She wasn't used to men who used the word "charming" in regular conversation, but he did have nice wide shoulders, so she'd cut him some slack. Actually, everything about him was attractive: dark hair, striking dark eyes, and what she'd define as an aristocratic face that spoke of a lineage that was Old World, probably Spain or Portugal. She had an admitted fascination for history, so she'd love to know his story. "I'll be right back. There's a corkscrew and glasses on the counter. Go for it."

He took her at her word, she discovered after she'd deposited his coat on the bed in the spare bedroom — one drawback to her quaint little house was no coat closet — and poured them both a glass of wine.

"Merlot," he told her as he set the bottle on the counter. "I took Kelly's advice and bought the wines I like best and didn't try to match hamburgers."

"She's pretty good at that sort of thing." Raine accepted a glass, looking at him as she did. "I've never had a business meeting on Christmas Eve, but you probably have. What's the protocol? I don't have a table in a conference room, but we could sit by the fire."

"I'm not all business, just so you know. Conference tables are overrated, and the fire sounds nice."

"I thought business was why you were here."

"Come on, Raine, I think you know that's not entirely it. I do have something I want to talk to you about, but I just wanted to see you."

Well, at least he was direct. She liked that, even as the admission surprised her. "The fire it is then."

She led the way and he followed, and as luck would have it when they passed the tree, Jangles decided on a drive-by attack to defend his territory. Maybe she should have issued a warning, but she was so used to the giant cat's antics she didn't think of it, and though obviously startled, Mick managed to not spill his wine even with claws in the hem of his no-doubt expensive slacks. She apologized as the cat unhooked and retreated back into his lair. "By the way, meet my cat, Mr. Bojangles. He has a perimeter staked out around the tree and he guards it. Sorry, I should have warned you."

"That's a cat? I would have guessed African lion."

"You should see the dog the Carson family gifted me. Mace made the mistake of suggesting Daisy help him pick out a puppy. She and that dog fell instantly in love. He's hers now. I think one day you'll be able to slap a saddle on that bad boy and ride out on the range. I have a sack of dog food in my pantry so big I need a furniture dolly to carry it in." In an attempt to be a proper hostess, she asked, "Shall we sit down?"

And get the business part done so we can relax a little. It was, after all, Christmas Eve.

Mick wasn't surprised at all by her house. Raine's taste showed, well . . . everywhere. It was so different from the elegance of his childhood home, he tried to restrain his smile. No settees, no polished tables, no

30

imported rugs or pricey oil paintings . . .

There was a poster of wine labels she'd created above the fireplace and the mantel was a hand-hewn log of some kind. A ceramic frog sat on the brick hearth, and there was a rusted antique toy truck on the other side. Her couch was ruby red and suited the dark wood floors, and a coffee table with a distressed finish added an artistic touch. A craftsman glass lamp patterned with butterflies and brilliant flowers adorned a bookshelf. Nothing matched, yet the décor oddly fit together.

He liked it better than his own perfectly decorated house, which he'd hired someone expensive to put together. Raine's house was comfortable and lived-in; his place might look like it was straight out of a magazine, but it was hardly homey.

"This is nice."

"This is probably about a tenth of the space of your house, but thank you," she said drily. "Daisy and I don't need more. She can get that at the ranch. I'm not really into personal possessions, which is a good thing since she acquired that enormous puppy. Along with my favorite pair of shoes, the rug in the kitchen has been a casualty. I happened to like that rug but I had no idea it was a culinary canine delight. He chewed it to pieces when my back was turned for about eight seconds."

He had to laugh as he settled next to her on the couch. "Slater mentioned every time Mace went to acquire a pet, someone else in family became latched on to it and he had to try again."

"It's like visiting a zoo," she agreed, also laughing. "The moment the infamous Mrs. Arbuckle-Calder became involved, game over. That woman makes an executive decision over whether or not you might need a pet, and if you are deemed pet-worthy, she'll pick one out for you and just show up with it and drop it right inside your door. You don't really get to say yes or no. How do think I ended up with the lion?"

He liked the way she kicked off her black flats and propped her feet on the coffee table, wineglass in hand. A gust of wind hit the rafters, but the fire balanced it nicely. "I wasn't allowed pets growing up. My mother was opposed to the slightest hint of pet hair in her house, plus my parents traveled a lot, so pets were an inconvenience she didn't want to suffer."

Raine furrowed her brow. "No pets?"

"None."

"Daisy would be desolate without her cat and dog."

He'd had some moments of desolation, too, but he'd survived.

"Everyone is different. This is what I wanted to talk to you about. I know someone who produces Pixel motion pictures and I mentioned you were a graphic artist. I showed him your work, and he's interested in talking about it. He's fairly sure Wyoming is the end of the earth, but he's willing to come here to meet with you."

She stared at him. "What?"

Raine had the most beautiful unusual eyes. Not green and not gold, but a starburst mixture of both colors.

"Pixel. Motion pictures. I —"

"I know what they are," she interrupted, groaning and briefly closing those eyes. "Oh man, I swore I was going tell you *no* to anything . . . but that changes the game."

"Anything?"

"Stop with the sexual innuendo, I'm processing here. I don't have the time in my day to add another thing, but I can't possibly pass that up. I thought you liked me. How could you dangle this in front of me?" She shook her head in disbelief. "I'm not even that qualified. I took some animation classes in college, but that's it."

He smiled. "My personal feelings about you aside, from what I've been able to see, you're really talented. I'd never have mentioned your name otherwise. But I'm glad I did, because the producer agrees with me. He thinks you could be a valuable addition to the team."

Raine glared at him from those vivid hazel eyes. "You knew this would be a graphic artist's dream. This is a calculated move."

"Of course I did. Never underestimate me." He had known. He understood a lot about being driven. Why else would they be exchanging emails at two in the morning?

"What kind of company are we talking about?"

She wasn't a fool, but he already knew that. "Let's just say you'd recognize the name."

She blew out a breath. "I knew you were trouble. I'm so busy right now as it is —"

"All you have to do is think about it and let me know if you want a face-to-face. I'm investing, so I want it to be topnotch. It's in my financial best interest to help him find the best artist possible." She opened her mouth again, undoubtedly to protest further, and he held up a hand. "That's enough business for one night, especially when it's Christmas Eve. I'm declaring the meeting portion of our evening officially over."

Raine blinked, then raised a brow. "In that

case, I think it's time for the dinner portion of our evening. I hope you can stand spicy food." She got to her feet. "Bring the wine, please."

"I thought we were having hamburgers." He followed her toward the kitchen, bottle in hand. "But yes, I do like spicy."

Her kitchen was as interesting as the living room. A row of unmatched antique canisters sat on the polished counter. The appliances were modern but the vintage hutch in the corner held what looked like a beautiful set of old dishes and pink crystal glasses. A mobile made from tarnished silver forks hung over the farmhouse sink — another piece of décor that was quintessentially Raine and suited the room perfectly.

His mother would undoubtedly faint at the sight, but Mick again found himself both charmed and amused.

"Good." Raine moved efficiently between the refrigerator and the counter as she set down a plate and several containers. "Green chili cheeseburgers are my indulgence on Christmas Eve. Questionably traditional, I know, but I love them."

He grinned for what felt like the thousandth time that night. "Are you kidding me?" he said incredulously. "I'm from New

Mexico. We didn't move to California until I was fifteen. My aunt and uncle still live in Las Cruces. I have done some self-analyzing to try and figure out if I go to visit them, or just for the food."

She gave him a surprised look that probably mirrored his own. "Are you serious? My cousin lives in Santa Fe. I love it there. She sends me the chilis every late August or early September and I hoard them like a miser."

"The real deal? From Hatch? Don't tease me."

"Oh yeah." Raine nodded, no doubt inwardly laughing at his expression. "I roast them myself and freeze them. I would save Daisy and the pets first in a fire, but I might consider going back in for my chilis."

He'd just gone straight to heaven. "You've just given me quite the Christmas present. If I can help, let me know. Otherwise I'll just stand here and drool."

She pulled out a cutting board from a side cupboard. "Somehow I suspect your culinary skills are limited to making reservations, but if you can slice an onion, you have a job to do."

"That I can do." She was right, he didn't cook often, but then again, he traveled constantly and home-cooked meals were hard to come by when one wasn't often home. Maybe that was part of what he liked about Mustang Creek — every aspect of the community felt welcoming and homey. If you walked into an establishment like Bad Billy's Burger Palace, you'd be greeted by name.

He hadn't even realized until recently that that appealed to him.

Maybe he was just getting a little restless in his life. Something was missing, and he knew he was in Mustang Creek for Christmas for more than just work.

Standing in Raine's kitchen, admiring the shapely curves of her body under that silvery sweater, he wondered again what it was about her that had caught his attention. It had served him well in the business world to play hunches and go with his instincts, and his instincts had started humming the instant he'd first laid eyes on her. Raine wasn't classically beautiful but she was one of those women who, whenever she walked into a room, unconsciously made everyone turn to look. Her vitality was part of the appeal, and since he himself was reserved and self-contained, he'd been fascinated from the start.

"Knife is in the drawer." She looked up and caught him staring. Wiping her hands on a towel, she looked down as a sudden faint hint of color bloomed in her cheeks. "What?"

"You're just so —" he cast about for the word "— alive."

"I hope so, since the alternative is pretty undesirable." The smile she gave him was quizzical this time.

He wasn't about to elaborate. "True enough, Ms. McCall."

"Knife is in the drawer, by the way."

"You mentioned that." He tugged open the drawer she indicated and found the object in question. "On the job."

Mick chopped onions while she dropped the burgers in the grill pan and in less than a minute, his mouth was watering from the tantalizing smell of sizzling meat. Outside, the snow was thickening, draping the trees and the wooden fence out back in a festive wardrobe of white. The whole scene was relaxing in a way he didn't often allow himself, a respite from the world, and the music softly playing in the background didn't hurt one bit.

Fire in the hearth, a concerto in the background, a glass of wine, a home-cooked meal and a beautiful woman . . .

The perfect way to spend Christmas Eve.

3

"That was a real treat. I felt like I was home again."

For someone who obviously hit the gym, Mick could eat on a par with the Carson brothers, and that was a high bar. As Red, the head hand at the ranch would say, he could really strap on the ole feed bag. Raine was happy she'd decided to make three burgers instead of just two because that third one disappeared quickly. Mick's manners were meticulous, of course, but he had devoured his food with flattering enthusiasm.

"I warn you," she informed him when she got up to clear their plates, "I learned all about how to make dessert from Blythe Carson. Ice cream is going to be all you get."

"That sounds just fine to me."

"Once you taste Bad Billy's Lemon Drop Ice Cream, you'll be hooked for life." She wasn't kidding. "There's a reason I don't dare keep it on hand all the time. That would be a desire to keep my girlish figure."

He gave her a slow once-over as he rose, plate in hand. "There's nothing *I'd* change, trust me. Let me help with the cleanup."

She'd argue, but had a feeling Mick Branson didn't lose verbal battles very often, maybe ever. He was the epitome of cool, calm and collected, with a good dose of masculine confidence thrown in. It was telling that she wasn't sure how to handle his obvious interest, because she'd decided a long time ago to just live her life as she wished and that her untraditional approach was a healthy outlook on life, at least for her. She'd sat down with her daughter and explained that the reason she'd never married Slater was that they were too fundamentally different for it to work out, and Daisy seemed to accept that, perhaps because she saw how much her parents loved her and respected each other.

But no one was more different from her than Mick Branson, so Raine had to question why, when their fingers brushed as she handed him the ice cream scoop so he could do the honors, there was an electric flicker of awareness between them.

He wasn't her type.

She was definitely not his type. She wasn't

sure what his type might be, but she imagined a cool, polished blonde who'd feel right at home in pearls and a stylish black dress. Someone who'd fit in at corporate functions and with the Hollywood set.

Mick interrupted her musings as he scooped out the creamy lemon mixture into the two Victorian glasses she'd inherited from her grandmother. "Daisy is a great kid from what I've seen. Spunky and self-confident."

She smiled. "That she is. It's hard to believe she's half-grown already. I don't know where the time goes."

He concentrated on scooping. "Have you ever thought about having more children?"

Raine's expression must have reflected her surprise at the unexpected question. He caught her gaze and for a moment she found herself trapped in those dark eyes. "I just meant you're a wonderful mother, according to Slater. You're young, so it just occurred to me. Plus I talked to Grace this morning and she told me her news, and also about Luce." He looked not exactly embarrassed but maybe off balance. "I didn't mean to get so personal so quickly. I officially recant."

Raine wasn't about to let him off the hook so easily. "I don't mind the question, but

41

turnabout is fair play. So what about you? Kids?" He was, she'd guess, around forty or so. There wasn't a fleck of gray in that carefully tousled dark hair, but Slater had once remarked that he and Mick were about the same age.

"Do I have any kids? No. Do I want them? Maybe."

"I feel like I don't know that much about you. You've done a good job of keeping your private life, well . . . private."

"Checking up on me?" He didn't seem to mind — quite the opposite. "I keep it that way as much as possible."

"I might have checked a little when you first showed up in Mustang Creek, but Slater likes you, so I trust you. If I didn't, I wouldn't be wasting BB's Lemon Drop on you."

"In that case, I hope to prove worthy of the ice cream. Sounds like a high bar."

At least he had a sense of humor. She was discovering she liked that about him.

There were quite a lot of things she liked about him. Too many.

"It's an honor, trust me. I don't just give it away all the time."

Without a blink, he returned smoothly, "I didn't think you did."

Raine couldn't help but give him *the look.*

"I thought I banned the sexual innuendos."

"Hey, you can take that remark any way you wish."

A man like him didn't look boyish often, but his unrepentant expression was pretty close. And those eyes . . .

"Just for that, I'm going to make you watch my favorite Christmas movie, unless you have other pressing plans."

"I'm all yours." He deftly wielded the ice cream scoop. "In case you're wondering — and I'm going to guess you are — my brother and his wife are in London for the holidays this year, my mother is in New York with friends, and since I have a little surprise for Slater, I decided Mustang Creek might not be a bad place to spend Christmas this year. I'm almost afraid to ask, but what's your favorite Christmas movie? Please tell me there isn't a lot of singing and dancing."

"Relax. There's none. I usually watch *Big Jake.* You know, John Wayne." She took two long-handled spoons from a drawer. "Not only is it a great movie, but it has sentimental value. My father loved it. I remember sitting on the couch watching it with him after my mother went to bed. Unlike you, she liked the movies with the singing and dancing and he needed a good dose of the Old West afterward. I was allowed to stay

43

up as long as I wanted on Christmas Eve. I still do that."

"You are a big girl, so you can do whatever you want."

She was just going to ignore that. He was deliberately provoking her. "I always have done what I want. Make a note of it. Do you want a cup of coffee?"

"That sounds good. It'll keep me awake for the drive back to the resort later."

The reminder that their evening would come to an end caused an odd sinking in her stomach, one she immediately chided herself for. After all, it wasn't like she planned to invite him to spend the night, no matter how attractive she found him. The softly falling snow outside might be adding to the ambiance of the evening, but her guarded heart was resistant to even the most romantic of trappings.

She believed in love. In loving your child, your family, and of course, she'd thought she was in love with Slater what felt like a million years ago, but that just hadn't worked out.

It would have been easy to accept his proposal once he knew she was pregnant, to settle into a comfortable life as a Carson, but she'd known from the start that neither of their hearts would have been in it. They were friends — she genuinely liked the father of her child and was grateful for the good relationship they shared — but that wasn't the same as love.

For the life of her, she couldn't figure out why it was Mick Branson who apparently inspired more than friendly feelings in her. She couldn't have picked a man more different from her if she'd tried.

Not in a million years was she Hollywood. Not in a million years was he Mustang Creek.

Though when he settled next to her on the roomy couch, ice cream in hand, he seemed comfortable enough despite the designer slacks and tailored shirt. He took a bite and gave her an incredulous look from those oh-so-sexy dark eyes. "You have to be kidding me."

"I told you. Billy is a burly, tattooed culinary angel."

"I might kiss him the next time I see him." Mick dug back in.

"And he might take exception to that." She took a spoonful from her own dish. The ice cream was smooth, creamy yet tart, and everything she remembered. Billy only made it once a year and she always put in an order early. Picking up the remote, she pushed a button to cue up the movie. "Here we go. The Duke."

"Pure Christmas magic in the form of an old western — sounds great to me. But I guess now would be the time to confess I've never actually seen it. Did you say *Big Jake*?"

"What?" She stared. "Never? That's . . . incomprehensible."

He shrugged. "If you met my family, well, let's just say John Wayne was not on their radar. I'm sure they would enjoy it, don't get me wrong, but they just wouldn't think of it. I believe I was dragged to a Broadway play as a child before I ever watched a cartoon."

That explained quite a lot. "Is that why you do what you do?"

"It might be. Why are you an artist? I doubt I'm going to get a straight-up answer. There probably isn't one."

She had to concede that one, so she changed the subject. "I can't believe you already ate all of that ice cream." He'd inhaled it. "Haven't you heard of an ice cream headache?"

"I've never had one, but for that stuff, I'd take my chances." He got up to go into the kitchen and she heard him rinse the bowl and considerately put it in the dishwasher.

Considerate? Oh no. That was trouble

right there.

Mick Branson was larger than life in some ways. So was Slater, so maybe that accounted for the chemistry simmering between her and Mick. She was attracted to charismatic men.

She savored each spoonful as the opening movie scene unfolded, feeling oddly comfortable. Even though he wasn't a stranger, they'd never spent time alone together before this evening, so the ease between them surprised her.

Everything about the way Mick acted said he was interested and she wasn't positive she was ready for someone like him intruding on the life she'd so carefully built for herself and her daughter.

His life was all about reading signals. Meetings, the stock market, international affairs, how the media was cooperating . . .

Mick was in tune with the business side of his life. The personal side? Not so much.

Raine was clearly a free spirit but there was a wariness about her that was impossible to miss. It wasn't like he didn't understand being cautious; he tended to tread carefully himself, or perhaps he would have had more long-term relationships rather than just a fleeting romantic entanglement here or there.

Her wary aura aside, he wondered if she had any idea how sexy it was to watch her eat ice cream.

He forced his gaze to remain on the screen rather than her lips. There was no way he'd take advantage of softly falling snow and all the rest of the ambiance to get her into bed, though he had a lot of enthusiasm for a night with the lovely Ms. McCall. Maybe more than one night, and that was food for thought right there.

He was afraid this was going somewhere, and Mick wasn't a man who considered himself afraid of all that much.

Luckily, John Wayne saved him along with everyone else on the screen. Well, not quite everyone, and with an analytical eye he admired the director's decisions on how the plot played out. It was his favorite kind of script, showing people as they really were — not all good, not all bad, but a combination of both. Slater tended to roll that way in his documentaries as well, with villains and heroes side by side. His characters weren't fictional, but balanced, and he made riveting dramas set in real places steeped in history.

"Good movie, but there's no love story," Mick pointed out when the credits rolled.

Raine sat easily with one leg folded under

her. He'd already concluded she did yoga from the rolled-up mat tucked in the corner, so the agile pose didn't surprise him. What had surprised him more was when her giant cat had wandered out and jumped on the couch with remarkable grace for a creature of his size, then settled down next to her. "Isn't that what appeals to most men? All action and no sappy stuff."

He shook his head, a faint smile on his mouth. "I think you have it backward. Men are more interested in romance than women are."

"Au contraire, Mr. Boardroom." She waved her hand in dismissal. "Men are more interested in sex."

"I sense a debate coming. Who buys flowers and candy and dutifully mows the yard just to please the woman in his life?"

She shot back tartly, "A man who wants to have sex. I appreciate a thoughtful gesture as much as any woman, but let's not get confused about the motivation here."

"You can't put an entire gender in the same bracket, Ms. Artist. There are a lot of decent guys I know who would never walk into the bedroom of someone who they didn't have romantic feelings for in the first place. Brains and beauty are all well and good, but if a woman isn't also a nice person, no thanks. I can tell you, in the world I live in, there are plenty of women who use sex as leverage, so it could be argued that your assumption works both ways."

Raine stroked the cat's head and Mr. Bojangles gave a rusty purr. "I'm afraid you're right and I was just pulling your chain. People are too complex to reduce to stereotypes. I don't understand a lot of them, but I think I know more good ones than bad ones. It makes me glad Daisy is growing up in Mustang Creek."

"I've looked at some land in this area," he heard himself confessing. "I haven't found the right combination of house and location, but I have done some research."

She stopped petting the cat, her attention arrested. Mr. Bojangles sent him a lethal stare for interference in the petting process, clearly understanding the interruption was his fault. "Really?"

"It's beautiful country," he said noncommittally. "I have a vacation home in Bermuda, but while it's nice to have sun and sea, I get bored after about two days. I'm thinking about leasing it out or selling it, and building one here, or better yet, buying a place with some history behind it. There's more to do in Mustang Creek than lie on a beach with a drink in your hand."

Raine looked thoughtful. "I'm the same way. I've tried it once or twice, but I can't sit and do nothing for very long. I don't find it relaxing because I feel I should be doing *something.*"

"We have that in common then."

"Why do I have the feeling that's about the only thing we have in common? Aside from a love of green chilis, of course."

"Not true," he told her, and gestured toward the TV. "We both like the John Wayne movie we just watched. We both like Mountain Winery merlot. We both would kill for Bad Billy's lemon ice cream. Mr. Bojangles clearly loves us both . . . the list just goes on."

"You were doing pretty good until the Jangles part. He's really picky. I can tell he hasn't made up his mind yet. He doesn't trust men that easily."

They weren't talking just about the cat, and he knew it. "He just needs to get to know me better. Let me prove how trustworthy I am."

"You want to prove yourself to a cat?"

"Well, he's a really big cat. I'm kind of afraid of him."

There was merriment in Raine's eyes. "His girth is part of his charm, or so I tell the vet when he starts on me about Jangles' diet. Luckily, I feed him, so he adores me."

"He has impeccable taste."

"I doubt you're really afraid of him and I suppose he must like you to come out from under the tree and sit this close."

"I respect his opinion, one male to another."

"That's a good way to handle him. Otherwise Jangles might boss you around."

Mick had to raise a brow. "Maybe like his owner."

"Oh, come on, no one owns a pet. Have you really never had one?"

"I always wanted a dog, but it never worked out."

She only believed him — he was sure of it — because of his matter-of-fact tone. He wasn't shallow enough to ever complain about a privileged childhood but his mother hadn't approved of animals in the house, so they didn't have any. End of story. He'd begged for a dog and the answer was no.

"That's too bad. You missed out. But it's not too late to get one now."

"These days it's a timing issue. Once I was out of college, I immediately joined a firm that sent me to Japan for three years. When I came back to California, I started my own company, and trust me, with the hours I kept I didn't have the time for a dog and still don't."

"You need one." Raine said it firmly as if the whole matter was decided. "Buy the land, build your house, and you'll have no shortage of dog-sitters to pitch in if you're out of town. I can be one of them. Daisy would be thrilled, and Samson is used to other dogs from being at the ranch so frequently. When it comes to the land, do you want real Wyoming?"

It was a generous offer about the dog, and an impulsive one, but he already had the impression that despite Raine's wariness around him, she made a habit of following her instincts most of the time — not in an impractical way, but just acting from the heart. "Yes, that's the plan. Real Wyoming. Solitude and a stunning view. A place where I can sit and read, maybe write something that isn't a memo just for a change of pace, and relax on the front porch with a glass of wine or a cold beer and watch the sunset. I'm at a place in my life where I'm starting to realize that being driven has its perks, but working every second of the day isn't necessarily good for you."

"Write something? Like the great American novel?" She was looking at him like he'd sprouted a second head.

"Believe it or not, Ms. Artist, I do have some imagination." He didn't add that he could easily imagine her soft, warm and naked in his arms, but it was getting harder to banish those images from his mind.

"I have no trouble believing that, actually. Excuse me, Jangles, your new friend and I have someplace to go." She gently scooted away from the cat and stood. "I'll get your coat, Mr. Boardroom. Time for a scenic Christmas Eve jaunt."

"Now?" He glanced at the clock, which had wands for hands and glass slippers in varying colors to represent the hours. Which made him think she'd designed it. It looked like, if he could read it correctly, it was nearly eleven o'clock.

"As good a time as any, right? Snow falling, the mountains in the backdrop and winter magic in the air . . . I want to show you something. No, now I *need* to show you something."

He had absolutely no idea what she was talking about, but was willing to play along. "Okay, I'm game."

"You might be when you see what I'm going to show you. I'll drive."

"Drive? Where —"

"Let's go." She opened a hall closet and took out a coat, then disappeared to return with his, pulling on fluffy white mittens as he did up his buttons. "This is perfect."

Mystified, he said, "I'll take your word for it. Care to give me a hint where we're going?"

"I'm a show-not-tell kind of girl. You'll find out."

Two minutes later they were in the car, driving toward a destination unknown.

The place looked as she remembered it the day she put it up for sale, but was also lit by the moon now that the snow had subsided to flurries, and she spotted the twinkle of a star or two as the clouds moved overhead in the brisk December wind.

Maybe fate had smiled on her twice this night.

Raine took in the weathered structure before them and tried to stifle a pang over the prospect of it being torn down. She warned herself that a man like Mick Branson probably wouldn't want the dilapidated wreck, and she could hardly blame him for that, but the setting was incredible.

"If you want Wyoming, this is it," she said as she parked the SUV. "There's a small lake behind the house, fed by a spring. It's so crystal clear, fishing should be a crime there because you can drop a hook right in front of a fish. I know it's frozen over right now, but in the warmer weather it's perfect for swimming in. And you have never seen anything so amazing in your life as the view from the back porch when you sit and watch the sun come up."

He was diplomatic, but she expected that. "The cabin looks really old."

"That's the understatement of the century. The house is falling down." She shut off the vehicle. "It was once just one room, but sections were added on here and there over the past century. Keep in mind the location. It isn't a lot of land, just a hundred acres, but you don't want to run cattle, correct? Just have a place to get away. Let me show you the inside."

"One hundred acres in L.A. isn't even a possibility. Neither is me running cattle, since I'd have no idea what to do. I do just need a place to get away . . . Raine, why do you have a key?"

"You can tear it all down as far as the buildings go, though I wish you wouldn't, but this is really a nice piece of property."

"That doesn't answer my question."

She sighed and turned to face him. "It belonged to my grandfather."

He paused. "Okay."

"And it belonged to his grandfather before him."

His jaw dropped. "You're joking, right?"

She wasn't. "It was built a very long time ago obviously. Don't those old pictures you've seen strike a chord? Slater featured a before and after of this place in his documentary. I have to say, he made his point about continuity across the generations. It hasn't changed."

Snow was still drifting down as she stood there, reminded powerfully of Slater's film. Mick said, "I remember. He didn't tell me this belonged to your family."

Drily, she remarked, "When Slater is in work mode, the rest of the world just goes away. Plus I doubt he thought it'd matter to you one way or another. Wait until you see the inside." She pulled out the flashlight she'd brought, the powerful beam catching the sagging facade. "No electricity. The water is piped in straight from the lake with no filtration system whatsoever, but since my grandfather grew up here, he just drank it anyway and swore it was better than any city water could ever be. I'd skip that top step — it was dicey the last time I was here and I doubt it has improved any."

Mick had a bemused expression on his face. "This has certainly been an interesting first date. Lead on."

She slanted him a sidelong look and hopped up over the tricky step. The entire porch creaked, but it had done so for as long as she could remember. "Date, huh? I thought it was a business meeting."

"I guess now's the time for me to confess that that was a ploy to get you to have dinner with me. My reasons for talking business with you were genuine, but the minute that discussion was over, it became a date." He was tall enough to step smoothly over the dicey step. "See how devious I am? You fell right into my wicked trap."

"Or you fell into mine." She jiggled the key in the ancient lock. There was an art to cajoling it to cooperate. "Have I mentioned this place is haunted?"

"No, but what would Christmas Eve be without a snowy haunted old cabin? If it wasn't, I'd be disappointed." His tone was dry, but he looked intrigued.

She liked his understated sense of humor. To her that was more important than good looks or money. The door finally decided they could come inside and obediently creaked open. "Here's your slice of history."

4

The inside of the cabin was like a time capsule.

Mick couldn't believe what he was seeing. Old wooden armchairs around a table made from what looked like an old trough turned upside down, an ancient washtub in the corner, a very old rifle over the hearth of a fireplace he suspected had been the only source of heat for the place. There was even a tin cup sitting on the table like it had been left there by the last occupant.

And everywhere there were books. In homemade shelves against the walls and stacked on the floor. An ancient dry sink was part of the kitchen area, as was a rusted metal work table and several shelves with some significantly old dishes. In the corner, a wooden bucket right next to it was probably the way to wash them.

Raine stood next to him, her mittened hands in her pockets, and said neutrally,

"No electricity, no heat, and if you look around for the bathroom, it's out back. My grandfather was a minimalist. He read Walden and never glanced back. Maybe you've heard of him. Matthew Brighton."

Mick about fell over. "The author?" It would certainly account for all the books . . . but really?

"That's the one."

"*He* was your grandfather?"

"Yes." She'd put on this cute white knit hat before they left the house and it set off her dark hair. Her nose was tinged pink from the cold.

He couldn't believe it. "My father had some of his books. I read them as a kid. That's how I got hooked on Westerns. Are you serious?"

"Would I lie?"

He didn't think she ever would. In his estimation she was probably as honest as it was possible to hope for a person to be.

He found himself grinning. "I loved those books. My favorite was *Paintbrush Pass.*"

She smiled. "Mine, too. Do you realize that was set right here?"

"Here . . . here? Like on this property here?"

"Exactly."

Oh hell, that intrigued him. "I knew

Slater's film emphasized the legacy of a famous Western author and it was Brighton. I liked seeing the town through that lens."

Her eyes suddenly glossed over. "This is where my grandfather wrote. He sat right at that desk." She pointed to the corner. "Impressive, right?"

It wasn't, certainly not by modern standards. But it was perfect — an old wagon wheel on a post covered with pieced together lengths of hand-shaved wood no one had ever bothered to finish other than to roughly plane it with a tool that gave it a moderately flat surface. Brighton's typewriter was still there and should probably be in a museum.

"He told me once that was all he'd asked for in his life. Solitude and a place to write suited his needs perfectly. Central air was an option he didn't worry about, he'd just open the windows. He didn't need a dishwasher since he had two perfectly good hands and that old bucket."

Mick walked over and ran his hand reverently over the surface on the typewriter, coating his fingers with dust. "I can't believe this."

Raine still missed her grandfather. He could hear it in her voice. "He was a rather salty old character, but all in all, a happy man."

"I can imagine. You know, thanks to him I wrote a couple of short stories in college that actually got published. My major was business, but my minor was English. I started a novel, but then I got that fairly high-powered job right after graduation." He lifted his shoulder in a negligent shrug, but life was full of what-ifs and he knew that. "Going that direction certainly made more sense at the time."

"This property would be a great place for a house." She looked him in the eye. "I swear you'd get a bargain price if you'd just let the cabin stand. There's lots of space to build. I've tried the Bliss County Historical Society, but they think it's too remote to really be a tourist draw, so they can't justify the funding for a decent road and maybe they're right. Not even Mrs. Arbuckle-Calder can whip up some support. I want someone to enjoy the place and not tear down the cabin. If you want a scenic spot, this is it. Just tell me you won't raze the cabin and I'll practically give it away."

So this was why she'd dragged him half-way up a mountain in the middle of a snowy night. He sensed from the way she looked at him that she was somehow confident he was the man who might be worthy enough to take on this legacy that mattered to her.

He had to admit he was flattered — and humbled. It mattered to him, too. He'd devoured Brighton's books, reading a lot of them in one sitting. He couldn't agree more that the place should stay exactly as it was.

"I'm not quite ready to sign on the dotted line, but I'm definitely intrigued. Second date? We can come back and you can show me the property in the daylight." It was difficult not to confess he'd see footage of it tomorrow, but especially now, he wanted her to be as surprised as Slater and the rest of his family when the documentary aired.

"Second date." Her smile was tremulous and he doubted that happened often with her. "I never wanted to sell it in the first place, but taxes are expensive. And though Daisy and I come up here for a picnic now and then, as ridiculous as this sounds, I think the cabin is starting to get depressed about being abandoned. I want someone who appreciates the history and doesn't just see a dilapidated wreck. If you didn't have vision, you and Slater wouldn't get along."

He needed to set the record straight. "If he wasn't a brilliant filmmaker we wouldn't get along on a business level, but he is, and as a person I like him very much. It has nothing to do with me except I help other people believe in what he has in mind."

Her breath was frosty as she blew out a laugh. "He'd so disagree. I believe he calls you 'the driving force.' "

"Maybe I am, of the funding of the production. He's the inspired one. It's collaboration, a sum of the parts."

"Slater Carson doesn't collaborate with just anyone. Take my word for it. I've known him for a while." She suddenly put those fluffy mittens on his shoulders and rose up to give him a light kiss that was very nice but not nearly all he wanted. Her lips were warm and smooth. She whispered, "I'm glad you're here. Merry Christmas."

At that moment a breeze brushed by, ruffling a stack of old, yellowed papers still sitting on the cluttered desk. Startled, he looked around, but the door was firmly shut and so were the windows. She said blithely, "I told you it was haunted. I think he likes you. Let's head back."

One of the pages had floated to the floor and she bent to pick it up.

Well, there was no question she was an idiot.

A sentimental idiot, but so it went. The minute Raine heard Mick Branson was looking for property in Wyoming, she

64

thought about her family legacy. That he knew her grandfather's name blew her away. That he'd read his books made it even more special.

Fate, plain and simple.

She was a great believer in spiritual signs, no matter if it was labeled *fate* or attributed to some divine power. If Mick bought the property, maybe he *would* leave the cabin standing. She'd resigned herself to saying goodbye to it someday, and Blythe had kindly offered to have the Carson Ranch pay the taxes, but Raine wanted someone to use the land, to enjoy the breathtaking views, to appreciate and find joy in it like her grandfather had his whole life. She'd thought about someday building a house on it, but it would have to be after Daisy was out of school. Their modest little house suited them perfectly for now.

"Two people have looked at the property in the past three years," she told Mick when they were back in the car and bumping along what didn't even resemble a lane. "Both thought it was too remote and the cost of bringing electricity and making a decent road was prohibitive. The road has to be built in order to bring in supplies for building and fuel. I'd put in a generator and call it a day. Internet might be a bit dicey, too."

Mick was hanging on to the strap on the passenger side. "How did your grandfather handle it? I mean, everyone needs groceries."

"He rode a horse into town. He used saddlebags."

"Of course," he murmured. "I just take the freeway or get on a plane. I guess I forget sometimes where I am. So he didn't just write about it, he lived the life."

"There's something to be said for convenience, but on the other hand, the middle of nowhere is pretty peaceful. There are sacrifices involved in both, I suppose."

"It's tough to get what you want without sacrifice," he agreed quietly. "I'm living proof of that. I worked very hard to please my parents when I would have rather have been one of those daring cowboys in your grandfather's novels."

"Those fictitious cowhands would have thought you were the glamorous one. Ranch life is cold, it's lonely, and you definitely don't get any thank-you notes from the cattle. At least in your line of work you get invitations to the Oscars."

Mick had the grace to laugh. "I wouldn't exactly call my life glamorous, but I get what you're saying."

"I never thought I'd say this, but I really see why Slater likes you. You're very real."

"As compared to being fake?"

"As compared to being a snob because you probably own suits that cost more than some of the pickups people drive around here. I'm surprised the cabin didn't collapse when you walked in wearing a cashmere coat and loafers instead of boots."

"There's a part of me that would rather walk around in worn jeans and a flannel shirt. It's all based on what we get used to, and what works for us." He took a deep, appreciative breath as he looked out the window. "Man, it *is* beautiful here. Aspens in snow are about as Christmas as you can get."

She smiled to herself. He'd mentioned the aspens. That was a sign.

It did look like quite the winter wonderland outside, the trees glistening and, now that the weather was clearing, a moon that illuminated the snowcapped mountains. Something slunk by in the shadow of the trees and disappeared before she could get a clean view beside the gleam of feral eyes. *Big wolf or small mountain lion?* Out here, either was a possibility.

Mick noticed it, too. "What was that?"

"Not sure." The increasing wind picked up some snow and flung it at the windshield. "But I'm fairly certain we'd just as soon avoid it on foot if possible."

He muttered, "Me, too. I don't see how the ranchers out here do it. Drake Carson in particular, riding fence lines after dark every single night."

"Not that I've ever known him to use it, but he carries a rifle and rides a really big horse. And I'm sure he doesn't understand how you're able to endure traveling the crowded L.A. freeways on a regular basis and having three-martini lunches in fancy restaurants."

Lightly, Mick said, "I usually keep it to just two martinis, no olive, just a twist of lemon." She caught his grin in the darkness of the car. "Actually, I tend to stick to a glass of sparkling water. I work long hours. A drink at lunch, much less three, is just bad for productivity."

"I might do business with a winery, but I agree."

"You see? We have another mutual philosophy. What time are you headed out to the ranch tomorrow?"

She turned on the county highway and it felt smooth as glass compared to the rutted, overgrown and disused lane that had never been graded in her memory. "About ten or so. We don't open gifts until the morning chores are done and everyone rides back in. Cattle still need to be fed and the horses taken care of, even on Christmas day."

"I was told dinner was at one sharp."

"My advice is don't be late. You've met Harry." The Carson housekeeper, Harriet Armstrong, was a legendary cook, but also an unstoppable force of nature. All three of the Carson sons considered her a second mother. "If you're late, you get to do all the dishes. Take it from someone who has made that unfortunate mistake. I'm habitually running behind, but not if Harry is involved. I toe the line around her."

"Don't worry, I'll be prompt. I'm really looking forward to tomorrow."

She glanced at the time display. "Today, actually. I'd apologize for dragging you out so late, but I happen to know you're also a night owl. I just forget what time it is. A personal flaw."

"You can get a lot done when it's quiet and your phone isn't beeping, and no one is sending emails."

"*You* emailed *me* at two in the morning."

"I didn't expect you'd be awake."

"I certainly didn't expect to get an email from you, either. Slater had some part in that, didn't he? I know you've never asked me for my email address."

"I asked if he thought you'd be interested. He said you were definitely a woman who made her own decisions, but if an animation film fell into your lap, you might jump on the idea."

"I see."

"There's a firm rule in business. It never hurts to make a proposition."

"Just in business?" She raised her brows, knowing it was probably more than a little dangerous to flirt with this man, but somehow unable to stop herself.

"Timing is everything."

At least he was reading the signals with unerring accuracy. She wasn't ready for a holiday romance when he would just get on a plane afterward and head back to California.

He wasn't serious, she told herself; he was just casually interested. She'd run across that before. Careless bachelors that came around, most of them shying away when they discovered she had a daughter, but Mick knew about Daisy already so she wasn't sure exactly what he wanted.

Mustang Creek definitely looked festive, with the streetlights adorned with wreaths and holiday lights strung in the windows of the closed shops. The streets were utterly deserted and no doubt everyone was snug in their beds. Her eclectic tree looked good from the street, she noticed as she pulled into the driveway. At the sound of the car, an indignant furry face appeared in the window, Mr. Bojangles monitoring — as always — her every move.

Had to love that cat. He was spoiled since she worked at home, but they were definite roomies.

"I think someone believes you've been out past your curfew," Mick said with a laugh. "He probably scared Santa Claus half to death while we were gone when Santa tried to put presents under the tree."

"Jangles wouldn't hurt a fly. He just looks fearsome." She'd invite him in, but it really was late, and he still had to drive to the resort.

"I won't argue that point." Mick studied her for a moment, as if reading her mind. "I had a very nice evening. Thanks again for the burgers and ice cream, and for introducing me to *Big Jake*. See you later today."

He walked her to the door and then everything changed. "By the way, nice kiss earlier but I think maybe we could go it one better." His dark eyes really could smolder, and she'd thought that was just a creative myth.

It was irrefutable that his kiss was more memorable than her brief impulsive peck back in the cabin. He was really good at it too, but then again, he was probably good at just about everything.

However, he seemed almost more off balance than she was when he finally let her go. He left without a word, getting swiftly into his rental car and backing out of the driveway, and she was almost amused as she watched him drive off. Raine went inside and sat down on the couch, Jangles immediately snuggling close. She remembered the piece of paper that she'd absently picked up in the cabin, and retrieved it from her pocket, wondering what it would say.

It was the end of a chapter.

The old man tentatively approved of the greenhorn, though he wasn't sure city folks were quite his type. Maybe he had real promise.

Raine laughed and scratched under the cat's chin. "You see," she whispered, "I knew Grandpa liked him."

5

For gifts, Ryder had been easy. Mick had once been a teenaged boy, so he had a fair idea of what they liked, but times changed. He'd opted for a gift card to a very popular online store.

Daisy had been more of a challenge.

He really knew nothing about a girl her age, and his childless sister-in-law was no help. In the end, he'd asked his mother's opinion.

"A purse," she announced promptly. "I have plenty of friends with granddaughters, not that I have any yet, so I will ask what brands are popular right now."

He ignored the implied criticism. "I'd appreciate it, but I can't pick out a purse."

"Sure you can. You have wonderful taste."

Well, he *had* asked, he thought as the call ended. The idea was better than nothing, which was all he'd had before. So he'd gone into the closest trendy store and asked the young clerk if she was Daisy's age what she might want. Directly she went to a rack, selected a purse he would never have picked out in a million years, and handed it over. "She'll faint over this," she informed him. "If we hadn't gotten a shipment in today we wouldn't have it on the shelf."

He took her word for it and had it gift-wrapped, along with some nail polish the knowledgeable clerk promised with a dimpled smile was popular with girls Daisy's age. For Blythe, a small Victorian tabletop greenhouse because she was the ultimate gardener, and for Harry, who always had a cup around as far as he could tell, a genuine English antique tea set. Grace and Luce were getting robes his sister-in-law swore by, since she claimed they were just the right weight, yet warm and cozy, and the Carson men were getting handmade leather gloves.

Raine had taken some thought. He wasn't trying to impress her; he was trying to show he was thoughtful enough to understand what she might like. In the end he'd stumbled upon the perfect gift — or he hoped it was, anyway. He'd found an obscure but original print of the infamous Sirens luring sailors to their demise when he was recently in Athens, the color faded because he had no idea how to date it. But the detail was so beautiful he thought she'd love it. He'd had it framed, and after seeing her house, he was sure it would fit right in. He'd liked her imaginative décor.

Packing up the gifts he'd had shipped to the hotel, Mick got in the rental car, checked his phone one last time, and shut it off. It was Christmas Day. London was hours different, his mother was in New York so he'd call her later, and no one else needed to talk to him in Wyoming.

The resort really was quiet, but Mick noticed the bar was full as he walked past, and there were a lot of skis in the lobby propped against the wall and a fire going in the giant stone fireplace. It made him reflect on how the season was celebrated, and if one person wanted to sit by a fire and another wanted to brave the slopes because the powder was perfect, that was the quintessential to-each-his-own. Both of those sounded pretty good to him, depending on the company. The Alps at Christmas that year he was sixteen had been an experience, but he preferred this homey atmosphere hands down.

He was very much looking forward to the company he would be in today.

The Carson ranch looked festive as he pulled up, the veranda of the big house decorated with twinkling lights and a garland, and there were two small trees complete with ornaments on either side of the doors. The row of cars spoke of a gathering in progress.

It was overcast and a few flakes floated down, landing on his shoulders and hair as he walked up the steps. Blythe answered the door, her smile gracious. "Mick, Merry Christmas. It's so good to see you."

"And you. I hope I'm not late."

"The fear-of-Harry factor is a powerful thing." Blythe took his coat. "You come bearing gifts. How nice of you. We were just about to start the gift exchange. Brace yourself for the usual male Carson competition. They are ridiculous. It isn't a monetary thing at all, it's just their nature. They have a built-in need to outdo each other whether it's through throwing a rope on a horse or buying a toy for a child."

"Hopefully I'll be a contender, since I made a few educated guesses." He stepped farther into the foyer. "But I make no promises."

As it turned out, he won the competition.

At least with Daisy. The purse was a leaping-up-and-down hit. She gasped as she opened the package and came over and gave Mick an exuberant hug, clinging to that purse like it was made of pure gold.

He made a mental note to thank his mother later.

Grace poked him in the shoulder with an accusing finger. "How'd you manage to find that? I tried to order one online three months ago. I'm still on a waiting list."

Raine studied him, clearly equal parts intrigued and annoyed. "Four months ago for me. Stop showing off, Branson." She wore dark jeans and a yellow top that brought out the gold in her eyes, and looked delicious against the sweep of her hair at her shoulders.

"I probably shouldn't tell you that all I had to do was walk into a store and there it was." He grinned as he sat back carelessly in his comfortable chair and took a sip of the smooth merlot Blythe had handed him. He had to admit that the spirited gift exchange had been much preferable to the stuffy country club dining room where he usually spent his holiday.

Both women glared at him.

Slater told him flat-out that if he would give up his shopping secrets, they'd be friends for life. "I don't think her first car is going to make her as happy as that purse did."

"I thought we already were friends for

life." Mick was going to go back and give the clerk the bonus of her life. The joy of giving was defined by Daisy's excited smile.

Slater acknowledged that with a nod of his head and a chuckle. "At least you beat out my brothers. For that, I'll forgive you. They would create a favorite uncle pendant and ride around an arena brandishing it until next year. Boys are simple. Give them a video game or some sports equipment and you're good to go. If Grace has a girl this time, the games will begin again. If Luce has a girl there might be an amusement park in the front yard with spinning teacups and a roller coaster."

Mick could envision it. "A unique addition to a working ranch. And maybe worth a brand-new documentary on how fatherhood can soften even the toughest cowboy."

"What can I say? We like to please our ladies."

"Having gotten to know your ladies pretty well recently, I can't say I blame you."

Slater caught his eyes drifting to Raine and said neutrally, "My wife didn't tell me until this morning you'd be here, but she was all too delighted to tell me about your Christmas Eve dinner plans. So how'd last night go?"

"Well. I told Raine about the animated

film. She seems interested."

Slater rubbed his jaw and laughed. "Not quite what I was asking, but that's good."

"She also showed me her grandfather's cabin. I can't believe she's related to Matthew Brighton. I've been thinking about buying property here, but it was pitch-dark so I couldn't get a feel for the view or anything else. You know the territory. Give me your opinion."

"That's so Raine. She took you there on a snowy Christmas Eve when there isn't even a real road to the place? You two could have easily gotten stuck there."

Mick couldn't help it. "That would have been just fine with me."

"So I gathered," Slater said drily. "As for the property, it's a wonderful piece of land but you can't run cattle there, it needs a road, there's no electricity, and that old cabin is supposed to be haunted now. That's nonsense I usually don't believe in, but I was up there once because Raine asked me to check on it and I'll be damned if I didn't hear someone say in a deep male voice: *Howdy, Slater.* I knew I was alone, so I about jumped out of my skin." He shook his head, chuckling at himself. "On the positive side, that lake is so scenic you could make a fortune just selling postcards and the view of the mountains just can't be beat. You'd wake up to bears and elk wandering past the decaying front porch, but when it comes to peace and quiet, if that's what you're after, you'd have it in spades."

Mick refrained from mentioning the sudden breeze that had swept through the cabin last night. He was also a skeptic but that had been an odd moment. He took a sip of wine and studied his glass thoughtfully. "I don't think I'd mind sitting on a porch with a cup of coffee in the morning and waving hello to a bear. I'd build a house with all the modern amenities, but the cabin would stay."

"That would make Raine really happy, but I think you just did anyway." Slater pointed.

She'd unwrapped the illustration and her rapt attention was emphasized by the reverence with which she ran a finger over the glass, tracing an outline of one of the figures. Raine was sitting cross-legged on the floor by the enormous tree. She looked over at him. "Mick, *where* did you get this?"

"Santorini. I was in Athens on business. I couldn't skip a tour of the island while I was already in Greece."

"It's gorgeous."

He held her gaze for a beat. "Maybe that's why I thought of you."

80

■ ■ ■ ■

Well done.

Raine was fairly sure that smooth compliment was overheard by almost everyone in the room. If nothing else, Mick Branson had style down pat.

It was unsettling to be under the Carson microscope at this particular moment. She was grateful for the extended family for both her daughter and herself, but the scrutiny that accompanied it was a bit much. Slater was fine, they'd come to an understanding a long time ago, and she was genuinely happy he was married to Grace. She loved Drake, Mace and their wives as well, but she wished they'd focus on their own gifts right now.

Instead, all eyes were on her and Mick.

She was keenly aware of it, and so was he from his expression.

The framed print he'd given her was simply priceless. No matter what he'd spent — and she didn't want to think about what it had probably cost him — it was the fact that he'd seemed to know exactly what she'd love that moved her the most. She figured she could forgive him the purse triumph. She was touched he'd thought of

Daisy at all.

Both gifts were the perfect choice.

The same was true for what he'd selected for Ryder, and everyone else; he'd clearly put some time into it, and no small amount of thought.

No one had ever managed to gain her attention in quite this way. It wasn't his money. She was fine all on her own. For that matter, if money was a draw for her, she'd have married Slater all those years ago when he asked.

Mick had read her grandfather's books. He could easily name his favorite, and since it was hers, too, well . . .

A small voice in her head said: *Watch yourself, McCall.*

"And now yours." She took a box from under the tree, wading through the sea of wrapping paper. Drake and Mace were supposed to be keeping up with gathering the discarded colorful paper and putting it into bags as each gift was eagerly unwrapped, but there was quite the crowd, a ridiculous amount of gifts, especially for the kids, and they'd finally looked at each other and declared jointly they'd pick it up afterward.

"Mine?" Mick raised his brows. "You didn't have a lot of shopping time."

"I didn't need it." She perched on the

edge of his chair, sharing it with him. She wanted to see his expression when he opened it.

Delilah, Ryder's little long-haired mutt, had taken a shine to Mick and was currently draped over his expensive shoe and his gentle attempts to dislodge her merely made her wag her floppy tail, so he'd evidently resigned himself to her adoration and the amount of hair being deposited on his tailored pants. Samson was having a ball attacking discarded wads of paper, while Drake's two well-behaved German shepherds watched with superior resignation, as if inwardly they were shaking their heads. Blythe's cat was used to the turmoil enough to doze on the top on the couch, having an afternoon siesta.

A man like Mick Branson probably thought he was having Christmas at a zoo. He accepted the box with a look of protest. "You didn't have to —"

"Give? None of us *have* to, we want to. Now open it."

He obligingly tore open the paper and lifted the lid on the box. His expression went from curious to stunned. "You're kidding. An original manuscript? I don't recognize the title."

"It's never been published," she explained

as he stared at the manuscript, reverently touching the title page. "Grandpa started it right before he died. *The Aspen Trail* was something he thought about for a long time, one of the books that run circles in your head, he told me once. He still used that old typewriter, so you'll find some penciled-in corrections."

He tore his gaze away from it to look at her. "You can't give me this. It's probably worth a small fortune."

"I just did. But, well, it comes with a catch."

"What?" He was understandably wary.

"Could you maybe finish it?"

"What?"

"Read it. I want to know what happens next."

"I can't possibly —"

"Put that English minor to good use. You said you have imagination. So prove it."

Harry emerged from the kitchen right then and saved Mick by making the grand announcement. "Okay, ladies and gents, it's time."

The males in the room rushed to help her carry in food, which wasn't surprising since they would eat most of it. And it wasn't like Harry just roasted a turkey; she'd made prime rib, Swedish meatballs, ribs, fish . . .

a variety of side dishes in order to please everyone, and Blythe had baked her legendary rolls, so it was quite a varied feast, as Raine had come to expect. Ask for it, and you got it as a special Harry gift. Dessert was a miracle, too, with everyone's favorites on the table, but then again, with all the leftovers, Harry would get a few days off to balance all the marathon baking and cooking.

Today, she also got another special gift.

When Harry sat down with the inevitable cup of tea, she picked up the envelope that had mysteriously appeared on her placemat during her last trip into the kitchen. "What's this?"

It was almost as much of a pleasure to see her open that envelope as it was to see Daisy sitting with her precious purse at the table, trying to eat one-handed because she didn't want to let go of it.

Harry's eyes widened. "A European River cruise? Airline tickets?"

"For you and your sister." Blythe smiled. "It's from all of us, so don't just thank me. You've always said you wanted to go, so go. I can manage this house alone for a couple of weeks and Raine is going to do lunches for the hands. Everyone is pitching in so you can just relax and enjoy. Take pictures of the castles, please."

"Stephano has volunteered to cook," Grace added, as Harry continued to look stunned. "I'm bringing home dinner from the resort's restaurant every night. You do realize he'll try to outdo you, right?"

"I'm making my famous chili on the weekends," Luce said. "In exchange for river pics. I hope you'll throw in some vineyards snaps for Mace."

Kelly piped up, "Yes, do. I'd like to frame one for the store. By the way, I'm in charge of dessert. If you'd leave out a few recipes I'd appreciate it."

"I will." Harry looked endearingly touched, maybe even teary-eyed, as she opened the brochure. "My sister is going to love this."

That translated to Harry loving it. Raine suspected Harriet Armstrong could be the most sentimental woman on this earth, but she was too stubborn to admit it.

Seated next to her, Mick whispered, "Is she a wizard or something? How many people does it take to fill her shoes?"

Raine whispered back, "A tyrant wizard. I believe that's her official job description. You've eaten her food, so you know she has magical powers."

He was way too handsome, especially

when he smiled. Hearts probably fluttered all over California, and apparently in foreign countries as well, since she assumed business didn't take up all his time there.

But he'd evidently thought of her on his travels.

"I agree."

"Why do you keep checking the clock?" She had to ask because she'd seen him keeping a close eye on it. Not that she was watching him or anything like that . . . no, not at all.

Right.

Mick just said in a neutral tone, "I have a good reason, and no, I won't explain. Trust me, it will be worth it."

"Promise?"

"Yes, and I always keep my promises. Just wait."

6

If there was one thing Mick knew, it was that surprises didn't always go according to plan. Still, he was pleased with the way his unfolded.

Dinner was over, the table cleared and the adults sipped wine. Snow had begun to fall again, so the ranch looked like an idyllic cowboy poster.

"Slater!" Ryder rushed in, waving his hands. "Dude, your movie is about to come on."

Mick smiled. It would've been fun to spring the news himself, but the teen's wide-eyed announcement added a nice hint of drama.

Slater, by contrast, was calm when he replied, "Don't call me *dude,* Ryder. I don't play on your basketball team and have the locker next to you. And what film do you mean?"

"*Wild West . . . Still Wild.* Your documentary. I just saw an ad for it."

Mace perked up. "Really?"

Mick hoped he was pleased. There was a short ad for the winery at the beginning of the film, and also an ad for the resort and spa Grace managed.

"Yeah, du . . . I mean, Uncle Mace, really."

"But it isn't out for another month."

Mick cleared his throat. The cat was officially out of the bag. "Actually, it might be premiering in . . . oh, about twenty-eight minutes."

It wasn't surprising Slater was visibly taken aback. "Mick, that's why you're here?" He turned to his wife, who was beaming smugly. "You knew, didn't you? And you didn't tell me?"

Grace, looking unrepentant, lifted her slim shoulders. "If you think I'd spoil a great surprise, think again. Surprise!"

"Christmas Day?" Slater looked floored, staring at Mick. "How'd you pull that off?"

"I have strings I tighten now and again." Mick wasn't lying about that. Those were some hard-won tug-o-wars.

"It isn't possible. Not for a documentary."

"Tell me that again in twenty-seven minutes."

"I just saw the ad. Like a major commercial!" Ryder was jacked up, his thin face alight. Mick could swear the kid had grown about four inches since his last visit to Bliss County and when he filled out, he was going to be quite the broad-shouldered man. "I was watching football."

So far the films had all made a good profit and that's why Mick could still get investors on board, but that ad had taken a lot of money and some true finesse. Everyone involved had agreed that maybe it was time to notch it up, especially once they'd viewed the film. They'd thought the investment would pay off.

"During a football game on a major network?" Drake wasn't a wine drinker so he lifted his bottle of beer in a salute. "Look at you, Showbiz."

I think you're the one we'll be looking at," Mick informed him, enjoying the moment. "Remember how the film opens? I think millions are about to get a peek at you kissing your lovely wife."

"Oh, hell," Drake muttered in obvious chagrin. "I'd either forgotten or blocked that out of my mind. Tell me you aren't serious."

Luce laughed. "Relax, you're not being rocketed into instant stardom, honey. In that footage no one can really tell it's us, and besides, they'll all be looking at the wild stallion in the background. I'm sorry, but I think Smoke is the one who will steal the show."

"He's welcome to it," her husband responded darkly.

Maybe it was the Hollywood in him, but Mick had always thought each of the Carson brothers would make a fascinating leading man in his own way. All three were intense, but he'd describe Slater as artistic, Drake as the quiet cowboy, and Mace the wildcard.

What was he?

Focused, maybe. Not artistic, that was for sure. Though he appreciated art in all forms, he couldn't draw so much as a square. "The gloves were just for show, Showbiz," he told Slater. "Your real gift is going to be the next couple of hours. I don't know how you're going to outdo this one, but you should have the opportunity if this doc goes over like I think it will. The backers loved it enough that the commercial was a sell."

"They loved it?"

"Of course. I held a showing. This is business, Carson. Don't look so surprised that they enjoyed it."

Raine was the one who elbowed him. "I'm with Slater. This is like having someone tell you if your child is ugly or pretty, Branson. It's nerve-wracking stuff."

He did get that. He really did, at least on an intellectual level. Defensively, he murmured, "He doesn't make movies just to make them. He wants people to watch them. Slater knows what he's doing."

"Yes, but no," she corrected. "He really does make movies just because he loves them. Having people watch and enjoy them is a bonus. But without someone like you, he could never do it on this scale."

Raine was an intellectual challenge at times. Maybe that was why he liked her so much. No agenda. "What's the point of doing it if no one sees it?"

"Because of the sheer joy of creation. I have artwork I've done I wouldn't sell even if offered a fortune for it."

"A private showing of those pieces would interest me a great deal." He made his tone deliberately suggestive.

Raine looked amused. "Please tell me you're usually more subtle when you flirt, Branson."

"You're harder to flirt with than most women, Ms. McCall."

"I'd like to think I'm not most women."

"You've got that right."

Her beautiful eyes softened. "That's

improvement right there. I'm going to help clear the table. I think we all have a movie to watch."

The film was brilliant, but Raine had expected that. Though she and Slater hadn't ended up on the same page in life, they certainly connected on different levels, and one of them was their mutual understanding of the emotional significance of vision.

The documentary was a love letter to Mustang Creek, taking viewers on a journey through its rich history. There were pictures of the old hotel that was there before the new resort, and video of a snowboarder in mid-air doing an Olympic-style flip, and then photos of cowboys digging a path for their horses out of the snow. Ranch hands around a table wearing chaps and drinking coffee from tin cups, and the same table a hundred years later, same cups, different men. The main street of Mustang Creek back in the day, and the similarity to the modernized version, including the wine store, before and after. Elk grazing next to cattle, the wild horses at full gallop, fluttering fall leaves and an eagle soaring above, a mountain lion perched above a walking trail . . .

And her grandfather's cabin, so unchanged from when it was built except for the slow process of aging. She drew in a breath at the picture of him when he was a boy happily playing on the steps, and later a picture she'd provided of an old man sitting on the front porch smoking a pipe — that child grown and weathered by time but still content. In the latter photograph there was a book on a simple table next to him; one of his, of course.

Her mother had taken the picture and Raine wasn't immune to a nostalgic moment. It was telling that even the kids didn't get restless, but watched intently. When it was over, there was a resounding silence.

Then Blythe began to clap, Daisy jumped up to run and kiss her dad, and everyone was talking at once.

The beginning of the film had been fantastic, with an unintentional shot of Drake leaning in to Luce for a passionate kiss, accidentally captured by remote cameras but, fortunately for the couple, entirely in silhouette. Luce had been right — the setting took over.

But the ending was astounding.

The wild horses were being herded off and Slater had taken gorgeous footage of the warrior stallion stopping to nudge a gangly colt, gently urging the youngster into the herd because he wasn't quite able yet to keep up.

It was so well done, emphasizing the continuing cycle of life.

"Let's hope the ratings reflect the quality of the work." Mick sounded optimistic, his long legs extended, Delilah yet again camped out on his foot.

"They will." Raine was able to say it with utter conviction.

Mick didn't hesitate. "I loved the idea, loved the execution, and Slater's style and his sense of timing are distinctive. I could tune in and know right away who ran the production. That isn't easy to come by."

"He's a bright man," Grace interjected, snuggling into her husband as he grinned and ran a hand over Daisy's hair.

"He has excellent taste," Raine agreed. She glanced at Mick's feet. "And apparently so does a certain small, floppy dog."

"Thanks." Mick eyed his snoozing new best friend, and the sleeping giant at *her* feet. "Raine, you do realize you're going to need a larger yard for that beast."

Samson had come over and collapsed at her feet mid-movie and, even at his young age, he already snored. His head was significantly bigger than her foot. She offered helpfully, "If you decide you want my grandfather's property, I'll throw him in for free. Problem solved. That's one big yard."

Mick chuckled. "Oh yes, I bet your daughter would let that fly. And I might have always wanted a dog, but I'm not sure about a rambunctious horse in canine form."

"Yeah, I guess I'm stuck with him. But there's one thing I can give you." She was impulsive and she knew it. It was exactly how she ordered her world. Follow the heart. If she had a motto, that was it. Raine took a breath and blurted out, "What if I just deeded the property to you on the proviso you keep the cabin as it is? Yours, free and clear."

It wasn't hard to see Mick was flabbergasted. He looked at her like she was insane. "That is the most ridiculous thing I've ever heard."

She stood her ground. "I don't agree. I think it makes perfect sense."

"Raine . . . the property is like what I'm looking for and I can afford to *buy* it."

"I believe I already told you that I want someone who appreciates it to have it. If you can afford to buy it, you can afford the taxes and to put in a decent road. Fix that top step on the porch, too, will you? Say you'll keep the cabin. We'll call it even."

It seemed like he was searching for words.

"You . . . you can't *give* a hundred acres and a historical cabin away."

The more she thought about it, the better the idea seemed to be. "You want land in this area, and you'd have it." She needed to make her position clear so she chose her next words carefully. "I'm really being selfish. Mick, I don't want to sell it. But I can't justifiably keep it either and let it fall apart. This seems a lot more right to me. You'd be doing me a favor. The guilt of having it on the market has been eating away at me. I think, given your friendship with Slater, you'd let Daisy come out there every once in a while to visit the cabin. That's so much better than a stranger buying it and not caring that he was Matthew Brighton, the author, and getting rid of it."

"If you get that animated movie deal I mentioned, *you* could afford all of that."

"That's a big 'if.' And I assume these things take time. I would have given it to the Carson family, but they really don't need more land. For them, it would just be taxes and something else to manage. They would do it, but it would be an imposition on my part."

"You *are* part of the Carson family."

He was right, and he was wrong. "My daughter is. I've been made welcome, no doubt about it, but there's a reason I spend Christmas Eve on my own."

"Not this year."

She held his gaze, remembering that brief kiss that was still a spine-tingling experience, the second one even better. "No. I want you to know I don't share my green chilis with just anyone."

"That was a Christmas gift all its own. If a genie had popped out of a bottle and asked what I wanted for dinner, that selection would have been my choice."

There came that heart-stopping smile again. She pounced on the moment. "So we have a deal then? Take the land, keep the cabin, and I'll make you green chili cheeseburgers every Christmas Eve if you want."

"Okay, we have a standing date."

"Mom, Mom." Daisy rushed in and flopped down on the floor next to Samson, who promptly rolled over to get his belly rubbed. Her blue eyes were alight. "Dad and Uncle Mace are going to take me and Ryder for a midnight ride in the snow tonight. Is that okay? I can just stay over again, unless you mind."

At least they'd spent the day together, and it was Christmas after all. "I don't mind." But Raine had to ask, "Are you going to take your purse on the ride?"

Daisy was appalled. "No. What if snow got on it?"

"Oh no, hadn't thought of that. It would be a tragedy." She bent to kiss her daughter's head. "Go and have fun."

"Thanks, Mom." She jumped up and ran off, and Samson decided maybe something was afoot and followed in a lumbering gait, clumsy but somehow still cute despite his size.

"Don't look smug," Raine informed Mick. "She loved my gift, too."

"I'd love to take credit but I can't." He didn't heed her request but looked smug anyway. "There's a very efficient clerk who understands both retail and young girls and does an excellent job for her company. Daisy should really thank her for the purse. So now you're free for the evening?"

What she said next might be life-changing. Raine thought it over — letting him know she wasn't *always* impulsive. She trusted him absolutely with her grandfather's property. Her heart was a different matter, because it also included her child. So when she spoke, her tone was cautious. "It seems like I am."

"Can we spend it together?"

"Are we talking the entire night?" She looked him squarely in the eyes.

He looked right back. "You just don't pull punches, do you? I'm talking whatever you want."

"I hope you can accept I'm not sure."

"I'm fairly aware there's a guarded side of you. Kind of like a prickly pear cactus."

"Those plants have beautiful flowers, so I'll take that as a compliment." She shot him her sweetest smile.

"I meant it as one," he replied. "I know you have reason to be cautious, and that you're used to being independent."

"I think learning to rely on yourself is a very valuable lesson. I remember as a child once asking my grandfather if he wasn't lonely sometimes, all alone in that old secluded place, and he answered that it never even occurred to him. He was happy with himself for company. I think I took to that mentality."

Mick regarded her intently. "You certainly seem to have done just that."

Maybe it was the season, because she wasn't usually that open with her feelings. "I'm not very conformist. I've met handsome men I would never give a second glance because they just aren't my type. I don't like them shallow, and I don't like arrogance. I'm not into cocktail parties and getting a manicure, but would rather mow my yard or tackle fixing a leaky faucet. That's not very feminine, I guess. If you're looking for someone who will put on a little black dress and stay on your arm at Hollywood parties, you'd better move on."

He just seemed amused. "If you think for a minute I haven't already figured that one out, you underestimate me. I hate to disabuse you of the notion that all I do is rub elbows with the elite, but I like quiet evenings in even more."

"Then how about a fire and a glass of wine?" She really wasn't sure what she was getting into, but it was going past the ankle-deep level and she might be up to mid-calf. "Maybe some philosophical discussion about life, and I'm sure Jangles will want to give his two cents. He might even think about sitting on your lap."

Mick lifted his brows in mock alarm. "I think I've had enough of animals sitting on me for one day." Then he added, "Otherwise, it sounds perfect."

7

He couldn't very well tell the truth, so Mick said neutrally, "It's certainly been an interesting trip so far. How's New York?"

His mother answered, "Busy, brilliant, definitely full of holiday spirit. There's nothing like seeing The Nutcracker at Rockefeller Hall. What was so interesting in the wilds of Wyoming?"

Well, he should have known he wouldn't get off the hook so easily. "A certain woman that, oddly enough, I think you might like."

He was sitting in his car outside Raine's house, gazing at her enchanting but unusually decorated tree through the large front window.

"Why would it be odd if I liked her?"

"She's definitely a small-town girl, an artist, and though I bet she could catch one without any problem, I doubt she owns a set of fish forks to serve the trout. By the way, thanks for the tip on the purse. Her daughter is now my biggest fan."

"She has a daughter?"

"She does."

"So she's divorced."

"Actually, no."

There was a judgmental pause. He expected nothing else. Better to get it out in the open now.

"I see."

"No, you don't. Raine turned down Slater's proposal because she thought in the long term that a marriage between them wouldn't work. They parent together and have remained friends. It seems like a reasonable arrangement and Daisy is a happy, well-adjusted kid."

"Slater . . . as in Slater Carson?"

"He's Daisy's father, yes."

"That's sounds complicated, Michael. Don't you handle a lot of the backing for his films?"

To his friends he was Mick, but to his mother he would always be Michael. As patiently as possible, he said, "He's happily married, has another child, and in fact, a third on the way. He cares about Raine as the mother of his daughter but he doesn't have an issue with my having feelings for her."

"You sound definite enough," she said,

but it was grudgingly. "I'll have to trust your judgment."

Considering he'd been a grown man for over two decades, he could point out that she had no say one way or the other — but then again, he'd always believed that it was a mistake to become involved with someone your family disliked. It added an unwelcome dimension to something that was supposed to enrich your life and make you happy.

It surprised him that the big, sometimes boisterous Carson family was comfortable for him when he'd grown up very differently. It also surprised him that he was so attracted to Raine when she was the antithesis of the women he'd dated before, and it surprised him even more that she seemed to feel the same way about him. He wasn't a free-spirited artist, or a tried-and-true cowboy.

"She's —" he sought the right description "— like a warm breeze on a sunny afternoon."

"Oh no, now you're getting poetic? It must be love. Darling, have a wonderful evening. Now I need a martini. Merry Christmas."

He couldn't help laughing at himself all the way up the snowy sidewalk, but he thought it was a good description and would stand by it. When Raine opened the door at his knock, she gave him a quizzical look. "What's so funny?"

He smiled. "Let's just say I think my mother likes you."

"Um, I'd ask why you were talking about me to your mother, but something tells me I'd rather not know. Come on in. Fire and wine are in place. If I eat again in this lifetime I'll be surprised, but Harry sent cookies and turkey sandwiches. If you get hungry, speak up."

"I will." He was certainly hungry, but he wasn't thinking that much about food and he had a feeling she knew it. He really wasn't like this with women, more pursued than the pursuer most of the time, but there was some serious chemistry going on his part anyway.

He was lucky that the lion didn't have an entire pride waiting for him. Mr. Bojangles barely let him get in the door before he launched a sneak attack, darting out from his super-not-so-secret hiding place and nailing his ankle again. It added comic relief that when the critter went back under the tree, his bushy tail was fully visible, even if his ample body was hidden.

"He must have trained with the special forces. The ambush was perfect, but he may have skipped class on hiding day."

Raine observed wryly, "He's not quite figured out that his size is a problem. I've thought about getting a bigger tree just to make sure he doesn't get insecure about his ability to be stealthy."

"That would be the compassionate thing to do."

She'd changed into soft, drawstring pajama pants, a flowing top with the same pattern, and slippers with raccoon faces on them. How that could be sexier than a slinky nightgown he wasn't sure, but it worked for him. There was a nice fire, and two glasses of wine on the coffee table.

The mixed signals were driving him crazy. He was invited — or maybe he'd invited himself by suggesting they spend the evening together — and yet she was dressed like she was going to a sorority slumber party. She'd told him flat-out she was unsure how she viewed things between them, but agreed to have him over again anyway.

The agreement was good. The rest of it was up in the air.

"What smells so good in here?"

"That candle from the local store that Grace bought for me. She knows I love vanilla." Raine sat down and visibly relaxed, cradling her wineglass in her slender fingers, propping her feet on the coffee table and wiggling her toes in those ridiculous slippers. "I love Christmas at the ranch, but a little peace and quiet afterward is nice, too. I always manage to forget how exhausting a big crowd can be. I go out to lunch with friends now and then, but mostly I'm by myself all day, at least during the school year." She smiled. "I love my daughter — that goes without saying — but the quiet is nice. Feel free, by the way, to take off those Italian loafers and put your feet up. *Formality* is almost a dirty word in this house."

"My mother would faint if I put my feet on your coffee table, but taking off my shoes sounds great." He slipped them off. "Solitude can be a friend or an enemy, depending on the person. I know far too many people who can't stand to be alone, almost never eat at home, and in general love the bustle of a big city." He relaxed, too, just enjoying the view, and he wasn't looking at the sparkling tree or the fire. "Is this the beginning of our deep philosophical discussion?"

"Or maybe just two people talking. You still worry about what your mother thinks of you?"

"I wouldn't say worry, exactly. But I try to

keep on her good side."

"Good for you." Her tone was approving. "I like that."

"Hopefully that isn't the only thing you like about me."

"No." She smiled playfully. "You have great hair."

He shot her a look. "Not quite the compliment I was angling for. I was hoping to hear my intellect amazes you and my charm is unsurpassed in your experience."

"Both those things could be true, but I just can't get past the hair. Do you have a stylist?"

"You think you're so funny, don't you."

She laughed, hiding her mouth behind her hand. "Kind of."

"No, I don't have a stylist. I get it cut and I wash and comb it. Surely there's something else you like."

She pretended to think it over. "Now I suppose I have to mention those gorgeous movie-star eyes and high cheekbones. Nice shoulders, too, unless there's padding in your shirts."

"And here I thought I wasn't in Hollywood . . . throw me a bone here." He was laughing, too, but also serious.

Her smile faded as she held his gaze. "I trust you are a good man. If I didn't, you wouldn't be sitting here right now."

It was exactly the type of compliment he might have expected from Raine — frank and straightforward — but he was aware that she meant what she said. "And you wouldn't be giving me your grandfather's property. We'll have to talk over that one again later. You really can't do that."

"I talked to Slater. He said it was a sound idea. Drake agreed and Mace was with it, too. One of the reasons I like you so much is that they all trust you. Those are some pigheaded, stubborn men, but they're some of the best judges of character that I know. And lucky for me, they don't even think about your hair."

"But you do?"

"In the context of maybe running my fingers through it, I do."

"Feel free." He certainly meant that. *Time to carefully consider your next words, Branson.* He studied the flames in the fireplace for a moment. "I don't think it's a secret I'd really like to spend the night making wild, passionate love with you, but that's entirely your call."

"Are you wild and passionate, Mr. Boardroom?"

"I was more thinking about *you* being that way. I've thought about it quite a lot. After making a spreadsheet detailing your personality traits and comparing them to mine, I've come to the conclusion that you are in the lead in those departments."

She almost spat out her sip of wine and swiped her mouth with the back of her hand, laughing. "Damn you, Branson, don't do that to me."

"Do what?" He put on his most innocent face, but he was laughing as well.

"We could be the most unlikely couple in the world."

"Maybe," he acknowledged. "But I never did like doing the predictable."

She set aside her wine. "I think your hair might be pretty messy in the morning."

What *was* she doing?

It could be foolish, but it didn't seem like that. Maybe she'd regret it in the morning, but Raine really wanted to lie in his arms as the snow fell softly outside.

And tumble head over in heels in love.

Not too much to ask, right?

Maybe it had already happened.

She had to admit that Mick was deliciously male lounging on her couch, and she'd never before been tempted to stray over the line she'd drawn for herself.

Nothing casual.

No males who would love her and leave her. That was for her own well-being.

No long-distance relationships. They didn't work as far as she could tell.

No one who would break her daughter's heart if he decided to decamp. It wasn't like Daisy didn't have a grounded support system, but still she had parents who lived separate lives and introducing Mick into the mixture was a risk. Mick could be all of those things. A love-'em-and-leave-'em sort, a potential scoundrel, as her grandfather would have put it, but maybe something else also . . .

"Do you have the manuscript I gave you in your car?"

"Of course." He looked like Daisy had when Raine had asked about the infamous purse on the snowy ride. "Why?"

"I need to see it."

"Sure, fine, if you've changed your mind about giving it away —"

"No, I haven't changed my mind. I just need to look at it."

He seemed baffled but obligingly went out in the snow and a minute or two later returned with the box. Flakes of snow glistened on his hair and dusted his shoulders. He set the manuscript on the table. "It's still just coming down lightly and there isn't even a breath of wind but I get the feeling it's going to really snow. I think they'll enjoy their midnight excursion."

Daisy would love it. Her sense of adventure had made her a handful as a young child, but Raine had that same enthusiasm, so she could hardly fault her daughter for her eagerness to experience new things and maybe take a risk now and then. "I would bet on it. She's a pretty happy kid and Slater is a wonderful dad." She gestured to the box on the table. "Pick a page."

"What?"

"Just pick one at random out of the manuscript and hand it to me."

"Raine. Why?"

"Because I asked you to?"

"Fair enough." He shuffled through the manuscript. "Any page?"

"Yes. Just pick one."

He flipped through the manuscript, selected one and shrugged. "Here."

She stepped to him, plucked the page from his fingers and read the first line: *He kept his emotions close, like a beloved jacket, worn and well-used, the one he would wear out into a howling storm. He was not a man easy to read, yet she trusted him.*

So she should.

Raine handed back the page. "That was

what I wanted to see."

"A random page?"

"It sure seems that way, doesn't it? Kiss me."

He'd fallen into a dream.

There was Raine, pressed against him, her mouth soft against his, warm arms around his neck and he couldn't be more enthusiastic about the idea. This wasn't like the brief kiss at the cabin either, or the more arousing one as he'd left the night before. It was hot, and he didn't need the encouragement.

At all.

What made her go from wary to passionate he wasn't sure, but he wasn't going to argue, either. She kissed him back with sensual promise and he didn't miss the signal.

He tightened his arm around her waist to bring her body more fully against his so he could feel every curve, every nuance. She did like vanilla. Her hair held a sweet scent of it, and was like fine silk under his fingers.

"Bedroom?" he murmured against her mouth when they both came up for air.

She whispered back, "I think that's the best idea you've had all day."

"You lead the way."

Her choice the whole time. This was what he wanted, hands down, but she needed to be on the same page.

She was. She ran her fingers through his hair. "Um, we do have one problem though. I'm not on birth control. I think I mentioned I'm kind of a hermit most of the time."

He traced the curve of her cheekbone with a finger and figured he might as well confess. "I have condoms. I'm not saying I thought this would be a sure thing, but I was hopeful anyway. Boardroom executives are master planners and always arrogantly anticipate the best outcome possible. I took two flights and endured a four-hour layover just because I was hoping for the kiss of a lifetime. I got it."

Oh, whoa, did I just say that?

"Of a lifetime? No pressure." Her eyes held a knowing look.

He was used to calling the shots, but she was definitely in charge. "Trust me, you didn't disappoint."

"Bedroom is this way."

He followed her. She could have been leading him off a cliff and he probably wouldn't have noticed anything besides the sway of her hips and her fluid stride.

As she walked in front of him, she took off that loose, less-than-sexy pajama top he found so inexplicably arousing, then tossed it down on the hallway floor. The graceful curve of her back almost did him in right then and there.

"Raine." It was said on a groan.

She glanced back. "Don't lag behind."

"Are you kidding? I'm following at warp speed."

Her laughter was warm and infectious, and he couldn't help but think that this was what life should be about. The joy of another person's presence, and definitely the magic of their laugh.

Raine's bedroom was a reflection of her personality, from the colorful artwork on the walls right down to the unusual black bedspread that was patterned with bright red poppies. The headboard looked antique, intricately carved, and he'd examine it later but right now that wasn't his focus at all.

Raine was shimmying out of her drawstring pants. "You seem kinda overdressed to me, Branson."

She was stunning with every stitch on, and naked . . . he'd dream about that image. Long legs, firm breasts, a taut stomach . . . heaven.

His hands had forgotten how to follow brain signals. Mick fumbled with the buttons on his shirt and finally got enough undone to be able to strip it off, though he was fairly sure at least one button went rolling. Socks next, then pants, and by this time Raine had pulled back the exotic bedspread and her dark hair was spilled enticingly over the pillow.

He even surprised himself when he said, as he joined her on the bed, "This is what falling in love should be about."

She brushed his hair back. "You didn't just say that."

"I think I just did."

"I'm so not ready for your direct approach."

He nuzzled her throat. "You aren't ready for us, and I'm not either, but I'm ahead of the game as I've been thinking about my options for quite some time. I can pretend you haven't captured my interest like no woman I've ever met, but it doesn't work. The first time I saw you I was sixteen again and my locker was next to the one of the prettiest girl in school."

"Do you say that to all —"

He stopped her with gentle fingers on her lips. "Raine, you have it all wrong. There are really no 'all.' I'm not wired that way. I'm selective. I always have been. Sex should mean something intimate and special between two people. If you think differently then you're not the person I thought you are, and I'm usually a pretty good judge of character."

"You know the right things to say, don't you?"

"I'm just speaking from the heart. Really."

She bit his shoulder lightly. "Then seduce me right now or I'll haul off and slug you. I don't know what I want long-term, but I do want you right this red-hot second, so you'd better make a note of it."

"Slugging is legal in Wyoming?"

"Probably not, but we like to make our own rules out here."

"I believe I just watched a film about the Wild West, so I'm going to take your word for it, ma'am."

"Hold on a second." Her eyes were luminous. "I have something I want to do first."

Her fingers ran through his hair again. How that could push him toward the edge, he wasn't sure, but it certainly did, even though he knew she was just teasing him.

Two could play that game.

He started with her breasts, firm and luscious, her nipples already taut, and when he drew one rigid tip into his mouth she shivered and let out a small moan of pleasure. He explored the valley between them with his tongue, gave due attention to the other nipple, and kissed his way downward.

She liked that too and wasn't shy about

expressing it.

He discovered she wasn't really shy about anything and that just tipped fuel right on the fire to create a skylight blast. The dance between them was natural and beautiful; when he moved, Raine did too, and the heat level started to scorch the roof.

Her climax involved a small scream and then it was his turn. He managed to remember the condoms he'd brought so carefully at zero hour, slipped one on, and then there was nothing but pleasure and deep satisfaction as he joined their bodies and sank deep inside her.

Mick had been waiting for her his entire adult life. There was no question. He knew it all the way down to his heart.

8

She was in his arms, he was in her bed. Jangles had decided to join them at some point and was sleeping peacefully in a large furry ball at the foot, taking up a good deal of space. Outside the wind had begun to pick up; she could hear the whisper under the eaves.

Raine was physically content, no doubt about that, but emotionally she wasn't sure she'd made the right decision. Mick had lapsed into a deep sleep, and was breathing peacefully, his tanned chest quite the contrast to the stark-white sheets she preferred.

There was no way she considered her relationship with Slater a mistake because it had given her Daisy, but it had made her cautious about choosing future partners. This man was far more dangerous because he didn't live nearby, and she liked him too much. Maybe gifting the property to him hadn't been an act of altruism but a selfish move to get him to spend time in Wyoming.

This relationship was evolving too quickly for her comfort. Mick Branson was a wild card she hadn't seen in her hand. How to play that hand was the real question. Discard him? No, he didn't deserve that. Up the ante? That was a definite possibility.

He was intimidating in many ways, but she was used to men like that. All the Carson men were confident, forthright and driven, and she was around them often. Mick was more understated, but he got his way just as effectively, even if he used a memo and not a lasso.

There was more than one kind of cowboy in this world.

She looked at Jangles, who sensed her uncertainty and lifted his head. "What am I supposed to do?" she whispered.

He answered with a very obvious reply by lowering his head and closing his eyes: *Just go to sleep.*

Sage advice. She took it by relaxing next to Mick and nestling in closer.

Snow. Overnight? Nearly two feet of it. Mick had obviously rented the wrong type of car. He had to admit he wasn't used to shoveling snow in L.A., so the waist-high drift by his luxury car wasn't a very welcome surprise. He wasn't positive a big truck could handle it, either.

He accepted a cup of coffee — Raine informed him it was something called Snake River Chocolate Peppermint blend, but it tasted just like coffee to him so he was fine with it — and he settled into a chair in her homey kitchen and took a sip. "I could be snowed in for a bit."

"No way." She looked cozy in a long soft pink sweater and worn jeans, her eyes sparkling. "I have backup. I *want* you to see the cabin in the deep snow like this. We aren't staying put because of a little snow."

"A *little* snow?"

"Hey, it happens here now and then."

It definitely qualified as the classic winter wonderland outside. The tree in her backyard was like a giant white sculpture. "You're serious?"

"I am. If it doesn't move you to see the place after a fresh snowfall, you aren't the man I think you are."

"What kind of man do you think I am?"

She put both elbows solidly on the table. "I've already pointed out I trust you. If I didn't, last night wouldn't have happened."

It was easy to say softly, "Then I'm glad you do."

"Me, too."

That was the response he was hoping for, and damn if this Snake River Chocolate stuff wasn't pretty good. He'd woken first and Raine had been half draped across him, deliciously nude and disheveled. The lion had been curled up at the foot of the bed and gave him the old stink-eye, but he interpreted approval there, so there had been a telling sense of contentment. Mick smiled lazily. "So, how do you propose we get out to a place that has no real driveway?"

"I have Alice for a reason."

"Do I even want to know who Alice is?"

"More like a what than a who. My snow-mobile. It's very handy around these parts." She daintily sipped her peppermint coffee.

"You named it?" He was amused but not surprised. Raine would do something like that.

"Of course. We'll go look at the property in the daylight and then we can go pick up Daisy."

It wasn't his usual mode of travel but he wasn't without a sense of adventure. "I assume you know how to drive one, since I don't."

"I was practically born on one. I'm a December baby. My father took my mother to the hospital on a snowmobile. I can drive it in my sleep."

At least he was in good hands. "I bet she enjoyed that."

"I'm sure she enjoyed getting to the hospital, either way."

"There's a valid point."

"How would you know? You're male."

No way was he going to let her get away with that. "I have feelings, too. Male and childbirth translates to helpless in most cases to control the situation. We'd love to fix it, but we can't always, and it makes us crazy."

"You all are crazy anyway, and what would you know about childbirth?"

"I lost a child once." It was the truth, but he kept it as low key as possible. "That was tough. Like you and Slater, apparently we weren't meant to be together forever. She got pregnant then miscarried. Our relationship didn't weather the storm. The child certainly wasn't planned, but I'd gotten used to the idea of fatherhood, gone to a few appointments, even heard the heartbeat. The sense of loss was acute."

Her eyes were full of sympathy and she reached over to touch his hand. "I had no idea. I'm so sorry."

"I don't tell anyone. But you aren't just anyone. I thought maybe you should know."

Raine was predictably direct. "Is that why

you asked me if I'd ever considered having more children?"

Was it?

He still wasn't sure why he'd asked that personal question out of the blue. He did what he did best and equivocated. "I asked because you and Daisy seem to have a wonderful relationship. I wouldn't mind a second cup of coffee, but I can get it for myself." He stood, cup in hand. "When's your birthday?"

She clearly knew he was deflecting, but went along with it. "The thirtieth."

He hadn't planned on staying that long, but maybe he should change his mind. "We need to do something special then."

"Like?" Her brows went up.

"Paris? Rome? How about Key West? We could watch the famous sunset over the ocean, and escape the snow. You choose."

No one should look so gorgeous in the morning, bedhead and all.

Mick could be stuck on the cover of a magazine in just his boxers and it would sell a million copies. She'd be the first one in line to buy an issue.

Raine waited until he returned with his coffee before she'd formulated her response. "Those are all nice options, but I can't just pick up and jet off with you, so right here would be better if you have the time."

She was touched.

In the head.

Don't fall in love with this man.

Too late.

"I can make the time." He leaned back and his smile was boyish. "I certainly have it coming to me. And it doesn't hurt being my own boss, I suppose."

"I work harder than most people I know and I'm my own boss, too. I don't think I could make the time."

"Sweetheart, if you don't think I work hard, think again."

It wasn't like she didn't know he did. This was a pointless argument, and probably one she was instigating in order to distract herself from worrying thoughts of love and forever after. She smoothed her fingers across the fringe of the placemat. "I know for a fact you do. What I don't know is what you want from our . . . er . . . friendship." She'd searched for a word and settled on that one, though as soon as she said it she was fairly sure a kindergartener would have chosen something more sophisticated.

Apparently he agreed, his mouth curving in amusement. "I think after last night we're a bit more than friends, don't you? I'm not positive what you want either, so we'll have to figure it out together."

He'd done a lot better than she had in the words department.

Jangles strolled into the kitchen and made a familiar sound. It was something between a growl and a screech. Mick looked startled and slightly afraid for his life. "What was that? Is he sick?"

"He wants to be fed. He's very vocal about it and emits that special noise so there's no misunderstanding. If it's any consolation, I wondered the same thing the first time I heard it. I assume, Mr. Boardroom, you can use a can opener? While you do the honors, I'll go get Alice. The food is in the pantry and the opener in that drawer right there." She pointed and got up. "I'd move fast if I were you. He can get cranky if it takes too long. I'm going to go put on my coat. When you're done, put on something warm and meet me out front."

"Cranky?"

"Very."

The smooth, urbane Mick Branson could get out of a chair and scramble across a room with impressive speed when faced with a large demanding cat. Jangles had his solid behind already on the floor by his bowl and his body language said he meant business. Raine was still laughing when she slipped into her favorite parka and went out back, wading through the snow.

The sleek snowmobile started sweetly. She'd gotten it from a friend of Blythe's whose husband had unexpectedly passed away, and much like her grandfather's property, the woman wasn't going to use it, but didn't want to sell his beloved possession. When Raine mentioned to Blythe that she was thinking of getting a sled — it was what her father had always called his snowmobile — suddenly she had one. The woman refused money for it, so Raine had done a graphic image of the vehicle and framed it as a gift.

She understood entirely not wanting to place monetary value on a possession so near and dear to someone you loved, but giving it to someone who would appreciate it was completely different.

Mick would appreciate the cabin property, especially on a day like this that Mother Nature had handcrafted to show it off. Brilliant blue skies, deep snow, and the mountains looked surreal, like something from a fairy tale. The skiers would be in seventh heaven, that was for sure. This was pure powder, the kind they lived for. Grace would be busy today, with the week between holidays and the resort always jammed full in this sort of weather.

When she pulled around, Mick was already on the sidewalk — probably to escape Jangles — and when she stopped he came down the steps and jumped on behind her. "Why do I think I'm going to need to hang on for dear life?"

"I like speed," she said. "Remember last night?"

He wrapped his arms around her waist and said exactly the right thing. "I'll never forget it. I trust you, so go for it."

She'd said the same thing. Trust was very important to her. Then he swept back her hair and kissed the nape of her neck just as she hit the throttle.

He had good technique and timing, she'd give him that.

Excellent technique, she recalled, thinking again of last night. Her burning cheeks appreciated the cold bite of the air as they took off. They were clearing the streets now, but not with big plows, more ranchers with trucks and blades, and they blew past without effort and were hardly the only ones on a snowmobile. The minute they were out of town she hit the back trail. Of course her phone started to vibrate and she fished it out of her pocket and held it over her shoulder. "Mind answering this?"

Mick objected. "It's your phone."

"I don't have a lot of secrets and it could be my daughter. So please do it with my complete permission."

He did, though she couldn't really hear the conversation too well, but she had the feeling he'd just met her grandmother.

Clara was not a Slater Carson fan, which was much more a reflection of her old-fashioned values than the man himself, and Raine had patiently explained time and again that he'd offered marriage. The opinionated woman didn't like the fact they'd slept together before Raine had stood in a frothy white dress in front of an altar, wearing a lacy veil and flanked by six bridesmaids as a grave minister made her repeat vows.

The truth was, Raine hadn't ever really coveted that scenario. An image of Mick in a tux flashed into her mind and she quashed it as quickly as it appeared.

"Tell Gran I'll call later," she said over the sound of the engine.

A minute later he handed back the phone. "She said she liked the sound of my voice."

"She *did*?"

"What? I don't have a nice voice? She asked me to tell you Merry Christmas."

This wasn't the moment when she could go into a long convoluted explanation about how her grandmother formed opinions first and asked questions later. Instead she said, "Look at that view."

The soaring vista before them was incomparable, and just one of the many reasons she loved where she lived. The streets of Mustang Creek gave way to a county road as they breezed through, and within fifteen minutes they were gliding along toward her grandfather's property.

Trees; leafless now but he should see them in the spring, summer, and fall. Even now their branches were decorated with white, making them graceful and glistening. The background behind it all was beyond imagination. The Grand Tetons were very grand indeed after a snowfall like last night's.

His arms tightened briefly. "You're beautiful. The mountains look wonderful, too."

Well, he'd survived feeding Jangles and talking to her grandmother — sometimes a lesson in patience — so she'd skip pointing out that that was a tired line. The man was probably just plain frazzled. "Wait until we go around the curve."

They crested the hill where she'd put the lane to the property if it was her decision, even if it was a steep incline and there would be a curve. Although the snowmobile was loud, she had the satisfaction of hearing Mick catch his breath.

So he should. The unobstructed view of mountains, a frozen lake, and the quaint little cabin could have been straight out of one of her grandfather's books. She was fairly sure the chimney needed to be rebuilt and cleared, since birds considered it a wonderful place to nest and over time part of it had toppled over, but it was definitely picturesque.

If Mr. Boardroom had ever wanted to be a cowboy, he could fulfill that dream right here.

"Raine."

"I know, right?"

"You could get a million dollars for this."

"I don't need a million dollars. I need someone who will keep it intact and let my daughter come visit. I need someone who won't develop it, won't tear down the old corral and won't destroy the cabin." She stopped the sled in a flurry of disrupted snow. "Call me crazy, but I think that person could be you."

9

The view from the Carson ranch was spectacular.

This view might very well be better, if that was possible.

Mick had to admit he was wowed. Yes, the cabin was beyond quaint with its sagging porch and drooping, snow-laden roof, like a framed picture of a holiday card you might pick up at a boutique and mail to your friends, but the lake and the mountains took his breath away.

Stately firs stood in stands sprinkled with the aspens that had no doubt inspired Matthew Brighton's manuscript, and there was no one around for literally miles.

And miles.

Taking in the spectacular scenery, sensing the peace that came from such solitude, Mick knew Raine was right about this place being perfect for him. He'd been thinking for a long time about a change in venue to

Wyoming, and certainly Slater's documentary influenced him, but he'd never quite envisioned anything quite like this. He could build the house of his dreams right here. They got off the snowmobile and stood knee-deep in drifts and he inhaled the quiet.

"Thoughts?" Raine read his expression perfectly. It was there in her eyes.

"I'm afraid that you already know what they are."

"Does it get any better than this?"

"I'm doubting it."

"You accept my terms then?"

He huffed out a breath. "Raine, you essentially have no terms. I'd walk over thin ice to save Daisy with or without the property, and your grandfather is a hero of mine. I'll leave the cabin as it is, of course, if you're serious about this."

"That will be all you need to do then."

"Why is it I think arguing with you is just a lesson in futility, but let me try one more time. This is exactly what I've been thinking about and then some, but let me have an appraiser put a fair price on it and —"

"No." She shook her head vehemently. "It's cathartic, giving it to you. Here, let me show you where I'd put a house."

They waded through the snow for a few hundred yards and then she pointed.

"There."

The spot was idyllic to say the least, with a stream that was partially frozen right next to it, groves of trees, and a level area with a view that would support a house the size he was considering. A big one. Wraparound porch, a hot tub in the back, second level deck, and maybe three guest suites. He wanted to invite his family, but also use it for business purposes, and inside he wanted the real deal. Log detail, soaring ceilings, stacked fireplace, ultimate bathrooms . . .

"I agree it's perfect." He wanted to invite her to live with him and that was telling of itself. But he wasn't necessarily there yet, and his spidey senses said she wasn't either, so he left it alone.

"I assume you won't go modest, so this would be perfect." Raine nodded, her cheeks rosy from the cold.

It would be. "Lots of space . . . yes."

Only perfect if you choose to share it.

Dangerous thinking for a confirmed bachelor, but the image was still in his mind. "You have artistic vision, so maybe you could help me design the house."

That brought her head around. "I did study architecture in college. Just a few classes though. Are you serious?"

"Unfortunately, make a note. I'm always

serious."

That was true. He could kid around, but didn't do it often or spontaneously.

Raine considered him thoughtfully. "If I have artistic vision, you have an artistic soul. Otherwise you wouldn't catch on to what Slater wants to do so easily. I would love to help design your house here. It's a dream come true for me. You'll still need an architect, but we could at least draw up the idea of what you have in mind."

We have in mind.

He wanted nothing more. "Let's do it together. That aside, this is my night. Let me cook for you. I'll have to borrow your kitchen, of course. I asked Harry if Daisy would eat lobster mac and cheese. She seemed to think that would go over very well."

Of course she argued. "Lobster? You can't get lobster in Wyoming in December. Last I checked they don't abound around these parts. The local grocery certainly doesn't have them."

"I haven't been in there but I'll take your word for it. On the other hand, you can get it if you know the right people." He tried to not sound smug and failed.

She pounced on it. "Grace."

"Not Grace so much as her chef."

"Stephano? He's making it . . . Well then, I'm in."

Such confidence. She was right, of course, Stephano adored Daisy so he'd been right on board when Mick had called. He said with mock indignation, "First you doubt the quality of my voice, and now this. How do you know I can't cook?"

Raine gave him a gamine grin. "I know *he* can. You haven't proven yourself."

Mick just gave it up with a laugh. "I can't cook usually but I spent a week in Maine when I was in college, hiking Acadia National Park. One of the rangers recommended this little restaurant and I had lobster mac there for the first time. The owner gave me the recipe when I ordered a second helping and she learned I lived in this godforsaken place called California. She felt sorry for any young man that didn't live in Maine. The recipe is apparently an old family favorite."

"My daughter loves lobster *and* she loves mac and cheese. Daisy will be thrilled."

"Can we pretend it isn't the only dish I can make?"

"Um, if you think you can fool her, think again, but go ahead and try. She's a smart cookie. That kid figured out the Easter Bunny, Santa Claus and the Tooth Fairy way before any of her friends. I'm proud to say she let them go on believing but she sure was on to me. When asked flat out, I cannot tell a lie."

"Good to know." He said it lightly, but didn't mean it lightly. Honesty was important to him. He kissed her cool cheek. "I mean that."

"I take it we need to stop off at the resort before we pick up Daisy. The road crews will have been out by now."

"We do." He said it with a straight face. "A lobster waits for no one."

Raine burst out laughing and picked up a handful of snow and tossed it at him. "Okay, now you *do* win for the worst line ever."

He reached down and retaliated. "If you want a snowball fight, I'm in."

"In that case, I should probably warn you I'm vicious."

"I have good aim."

Raine pelted him with another snowball. "Good luck, cowboy. I was born in snow country."

He needed luck. She was pretty accurate as well. After the third one caught him right in the chest he surrendered, arms in the air. "Mercy."

Of course she pelted him again.

He tackled her and the resulting kiss made

him forget about the cold even though they were both lying in the snow.

"I'm falling in love with you." He definitely hadn't meant to admit that, but it was true and she already knew it.

"If you haven't figured out we have the same problem, then you aren't paying attention." Raine looked reflective lying beneath him. "We're both idiots."

"I don't think I am."

"I don't think I am, either." Her eyes were suddenly shiny. "But I've been wrong before."

"Raine, do you really think Slater was a mistake?"

She sat up and shook snow out of her dark hair. "No, of course not. I wouldn't have Daisy if it wasn't for him, and I'll always care about him. It's just that I keep hoping to find gold in a muddy river bed, but I haven't had a strike yet."

He probably had snow in his hair as well but didn't care. "You sure about that? I'm going to finish that manuscript, by the way. I don't know if I can do it justice, but maybe *I'll* get a strike."

She kissed him then, snowy mittens on his cheeks but her mouth was warm and giving. "I'm so glad."

"I won't know what I'm doing."

"You'll do great. I feel it."

"I'll trust you to tell me if it's terrible."

"Oh, don't you think you'd be the first to know?" Raine gave him a merry glance before getting to her feet. "I'm not shy with my opinions in case you haven't noticed. I believe *blatantly outspoken* is the Carsons' preferred term for me. I have bad news for you, though. Their head ranch hand, Red, is a die-hard Matthew Brighton fan. It's his opinion you really need to worry about, because he won't pull his punches if you can't tell a snake hole from the Grand Canyon."

"Great. Well, I guess I know who my expert consultant will be if I need help with research." Mick got up also and tried to brush off his jeans. "I'm probably nuts even to try this, but I do like a challenge."

The look she gave him was only half-teasing. "Is that why you fell for me? Because I'm a challenge?"

"Maybe it started that way," he admitted, catching her hand as they made their way back to the snowmobile. "You do keep me on my toes. But if you haven't figured out that I'm crazy about everything that makes you you, then you're the one who's not paying attention."

"Likewise, cowboy." She started the snowmobile again. "Climb on board. Isn't there a lobster with your name on it?"

Cream, cheese, pasta, garlic . . . there was no way to go wrong with a meal like that, so Mick was cheating. He did let Raine do the salad and got the bread from the restaurant, but otherwise he prepared everything himself. And if the purse he'd given Daisy had won her over, the dinner he served them made her his devoted fan for life.

That was so important to her, Raine thought as she watched her daughter interact so naturally with Mick. Daisy's face was animated as she described the midnight ride in the snow, and she'd definitely cleaned her plate so his dinner choice had been about as popular as Harry's cooking, which was saying something.

Clever man.

"Remind me to kiss Stephano next time I see him," Raine declared during a lull in the excited conversation. "That lobster was the perfect touch."

"How about you kiss the actual cook, not just the ingredient-supplier?" Mick gave her a look of mock reproof. "Besides, I'm way better looking than he is."

"Maybe a tinge." Raine gave him a dreamy

smile. "But he has that Latin air, you know?"

Daisy joined her mother in giggling at the expression on Mick's face. Raine knew she was taking it all in — their unexpected guest, the overt affection between them. What Raine wanted her daughter to walk away with from tonight was a sense that love was supposed to be fun. It wasn't supposed to be easy all of the time, but fun was very important.

Mick threw up his hands. "In that case, how's an ordinary guy supposed to compete?"

She shouldn't say it so softly, but she did anyway. "Oh you aren't ordinary by any means."

"No?"

"No."

Enough said. Daisy was clearly paying attention to the nuances of the conversation, listening avidly. The good news was that purse aside, she seemed to really like Mick. That hadn't been the case last time she'd introduced her daughter to a man she'd briefly been dating, a doctor from a nearby town. Daisy had instantly pronounced him boring and that put an end to that. She might not have known him long enough to give him a fair shot, but Raine trusted her daughter's instincts. Besides that, any man who was a part of her life would be part of her daughter's as well. Her opinion counted.

Daisy jumped up. "Who wants ice cream? I'll get it." She began to eagerly stack the plates. They had an agreement. Raine cooked and cleaned up the kitchen, but Daisy cleared the table.

"Her grandmother is Blythe Carson," Raine confided. "According to Blythe, ice cream is an essential food group all by itself. Beware."

Mick lifted a brow. "Beware? I love ice cream."

"Good. Get ready to prove it."

He ended up with brownie fudge with cherries and marshmallow topping in a massive bowl, not to mention various kinds of sprinkles in rainbow colors. Before he dug in he muttered, "Beware. Now I get it. I'll have to go to the gym fifteen times to work this off."

"I'll go with you." Her bowl was half the size.

"You can go with me anywhere."

There was that smooth Hollywood charm again. She scooped up marshmallow and cherry on her spoon. "You see, our problem is I'm *not* going anywhere. I can't. That's why I want to contact my Realtor's office the minute it's open, yank the cabin property off the market, and tell them to set up a closing."

"Cabin? You mean Grandpa's house?" Daisy had seemed to be focused on her own heaping spoonful, but Raine knew she was listening to their every word.

"That's right. I'm giving it to Mick."

"That's a pretty good idea."

Raine smiled. "Mick is a writer. He'll love it there."

That was a full-out dare. Daisy actually stopped eating ice cream, and that was something. Her eyes were wide. "You are? Like him?"

He blinked. "No." Then relented. "Well, I'm afraid I'm nowhere near as talented as your great-grandfather, but I've tried a time or two."

"He's been published in literary magazines." Raine couldn't resist imparting that information and ignored the quelling look from the man across the table. "And he's read the Matthew Brighton books."

"Have you really?" Daisy grinned, obviously delighted. "My favorite is *Mountain Sunrise.*"

"I liked that one, too." Mick acted nonchalant, but Raine sensed his passion for finishing the manuscript. No matter how it turned out, she was glad to have played a small role in encouraging him to explore the creative side he didn't often get to give free rein to.

Raine got up. "I'm going to go clean the kitchen. I truly can't eat another bite. I might need to go for a walk but someone should probably carry me."

Daisy pointed out, "Then it wouldn't be a walk."

"I'll help you clean up since I made the mess, and then I'll take you on that walk." Mick rose as well. "Beautiful moon out there."

Raine probably should have predicted the total chaos that ensued when Mick took a step toward the kitchen.

Jangles did a daring guerilla move and went for his ankles, but now Samson was back in residence and wanted part of the action. Raine was almost swept off her feet — not in the romantic sense — as a giant puppy chased a giant cat and both of them nearly took her out, the cat dodging right in front of her and the dog accidentally slamming into the back of her legs. Mick managed to keep his balance during the mayhem and caught her shoulders, steadying her at the last second as the animals dashed past.

"Such a peaceful household," she said darkly. "Bunch of wild critters that don't realize if they break your leg you can't get to the grocery store to buy them more food."

They went by again at full speed, careening into walls and not caring, playing a classic game of circling the house. It was endearingly funny, but she made sure her computer wasn't plugged in when they really got going because Samson could easily catch that cord. One day he might not be so clumsy, but for now she was taking precautions.

"I like it," Mick said and kissed her swiftly out of Daisy's sightline. "Full of life. I'm starting to think my house in California is entirely too quiet."

"Then move here. I promise no peace and quiet at all."

She was really losing it if she'd just said that. So she just blundered on. "You can't live in the cabin while the house is being built."

"Sure I could. I've also read Walden."

"You wear Italian shoes."

"So? Stop harping on my shoes and focus on the man." He caught her playfully around the waist. "But invitation accepted.

Where would I sleep? With you?"

"I'm thinking that might be the case." She went serious because she might as well make her position clear. "But only on the nights when Daisy is at the ranch. I'm not so naive as to think she hasn't cottoned on to the fact that there's something going between us, but I also know Slater and Grace kept their feelings for each other off her radar until they understood where they were headed, and I appreciated that. Daisy likes you, and so do I —"

"Glad to hear it." He was busy nuzzling her neck. "I can always stay at the cabin."

"Don't you have business on the West Coast?"

"That's the beauty of modern technology. I can work from anywhere, to a certain extent." He kissed her again.

"No plumbing." She whispered it against his mouth, not quite sure why she was trying to warn him off when she so badly wanted him to stay.

"Versus no you? That's hardly a contest."

"I have to think of my daughter."

"I will always think of her, too, I promise. And then there's the other females in our lives to think of. We'll have to handle my mother and your grandmother, Blythe, Harry, and the rest of the bunch."

"The interferers. Grace, Luce and Kelly will be just as bad."

"Exactly."

She couldn't help but laugh at his grim expression. "They'll be fine. They interfere, but mean well."

"Women just don't operate like men."

"Do you think?"

His grin was instant. "Think? Your presence seems to impair the process. No offense intended."

"None taken." She disengaged from his embrace. "If you can rinse dishes and hand them to me while I load the dishwasher, I'll be yours for life."

"Hey, I thought I was the one that made the deals. Don't try and show me up." He picked up a plate and flipped the lever on the faucet. "Obviously I accept your terms. We can negotiate the details."

10

The skiers were out in full force and Mick sat in a comfortable chair and watched out the window of his room as they careened down the slopes while he sipped a cup of coffee. It was clear and brilliant outside and he was in a reflective mood, watching the sunlight bounce off the sparkling snow.

I'll be yours for life.

Now that was a thought.

She'd probably meant it in a different way than he took it, joking, not serious at all, but it had certainly struck a nerve.

He sat there and seriously considered marriage for the first time in his life.

That word had always scared him. It wasn't the permanence of it, since half the people he knew were divorced — it was the emotional investment. Yet the true problem was that he was convinced it scared Raine even more. She'd opted out once already. Slater was a great guy but she'd given him a firm no when he proposed, and changing her mind was going to take more than the two of them enjoying a night in bed together.

So he really considered it over a second cup of coffee, and then called his brother. Ran answered pretty swiftly but he lived by his phone, even at this time of the year. Mick said, "Hi. How's London?"

"Covered in white. Snowed last night. How's Wyoming?"

"Ditto."

"An ocean away and the same story. It must be Christmas. So what's up?"

"I think I need a ring and Ingrid is no slouch in that department. Could you ask her to pick one out? I'll write you a check when you're back in the States, or I can send you the money now. We can get it sized here."

His brother's wife had been a jewelry store buyer before the two of them got married and remained a consummate gem shopper. They kept her jewelry in a safe.

"What kind of ring?"

"Engagement."

"Are you joking around?" Ran sounded stunned. "*You're* proposing to someone?"

"I'm going to give it a try. And if she says yes, moving to Wyoming full-time. I do half my business by phone or email, not to mention I have to fly from Los Angeles all the time anyway for meetings. I can do that from here."

"You'd *live* in Wyoming?"

He chuckled at his brother's horrified tone. "I realize Mustang Creek doesn't have a ballet company or symphony orchestra, but the scenery alone makes up for that, and yes, I'd live here because she's here and isn't going anywhere and I wouldn't ask it of her. I like it here anyway, you know that."

"I know you keep going back and now I finally understand why."

He thought about Bad Billy's Burger Palace and Harry's cooking, not to mention the resort. "Lots of good food choices, great schools, all the peace and quiet a man could want, and I doubt the sunsets could be beat by any place on earth. No shortage of beautiful women, either." Grace, Luce, and Kelly certainly qualified, as did the wives of Slater's friends he'd met. Not that he had eyes for anyone but Raine. "And I'm talking the type that don't need a salon and expensive make-up artist to make it happen."

His brother wasn't without a sense of humor. "I might just visit then, to check out the scenery."

"You'll be welcome anytime. Tell Ingrid

that Raine would probably like something different for the ring. She's an artist. I don't think she'd go for a two-carat marquis. She might turn me down on that one. Something really eclectic would work. Tell Ingrid I implicitly trust her and Raine has hazel eyes and dark hair."

Randal Branson had never been all that imaginative. "The color of her hair and eyes matters . . . why?"

"I have no idea, but I figure it doesn't hurt to arm Ingrid with enough information to find the perfect ring. Tell her to make it unusual, one of a kind even. Just like Raine."

"I thought the romantic ideal was the man should pick out the ring."

He wasn't easily fooled. "Who picked out Ingrid's? I've seen it. It's tasteful, so don't try to claim it was you."

"Okay, you got me. She chose it herself and I was happy to let her."

"I rest my case," Mick said. "You'll bring the ring back from London?"

"Ingrid has a lot of associates here. I think she'll enjoy shopping for it and be really picky about the stone and setting. I've seen her in action. We fly back tomorrow and she wants to do some last-minute shopping so we were going out anyway. We're invited to the Austins' famous annual New Year's party."

Mick had been, too, but he was spending the holiday right where he was. Those glitzy affairs had lost their gloss even before he'd become so involved with Raine.

"I was thinking New Year's Eve is the perfect night to propose."

"Not waiting around."

"I thought you'd just intimated I'd waited around too much in my life already."

"I'm just happy for you." Ran sounded sincere. "Ingrid will find you the perfect ring and I'll have it insured and overnighted."

"That's all I could ask for. Tell Ingrid thanks in advance from me."

They ended the call and he settled back, amazingly content with his decision. He was used to such a fast-paced life he found he liked just sitting there and watching the ski runs. It was interesting to take time to contemplate the life-changing curve in the road of his future.

He'd have an instant daughter if Raine said yes. Maybe more children; a subject they would need to discuss later.

If she said yes.

It would certainly affect the plans for the house he was going to build.

If she said yes.

It was going to completely change his life.
If she said yes.

Not a given.

Suddenly restless, he got up to pace the length of the room. He'd always considered himself more a man of controlled contemplation than action, but right now he needed to walk off this unexpected insecurity. It was probably a good sign it meant so much to him, but he wasn't enjoying the myriad emotions. He was nervous, a concept that was foreign to him. Usually, when awaiting the outcome of a deal he'd negotiated, he was confident and straightforward, and if it fell through — which happened now and then for various reasons — so it went.

He couldn't shrug this off if Raine decided he wasn't the one.

The break-up after the miscarriage had been painful, but they would probably have only stayed together for the baby, so that was something else he and Raine had in common. Like Slater, he would have offered marriage, but if his ex-girlfriend had said yes, he wasn't sure at all it would have lasted. The experience did teach him something about himself and that was that he was much more traditional than he thought, but it also made him realize he valued relationships in a long-term way.

Double-whammy right there.

He wanted a wife, family, and roots.

Speaking of roots . . . if he was going to make good on his promise, he might as well get started on reading *The Aspen Trail.* What better way to spend a snowy morning, especially since he knew Raine was working, though she'd agreed to lunch. She'd already had plans to meet with friends for dinner. They sponsored a college scholarship at the local high school and between them formed a committee each year to review the applications and select a recipient. The Carson Ranch matched their contributions and people from all over the state applied for it, and Raine had said with a definite tinge of emotion in her voice that it was wonderful to support higher education. He agreed. Already it had occurred to him to maybe set up a college fund for Daisy in her grandfather's name to offset the property gift.

So he sat back down, told himself to forget everything else for the moment, and he started to read.

CHAPTER ONE

The haze of the sun hit the leaves in a slanted light and cast shadows on the ground. The cowboy nudged his horse

forward with his heel, the silent com-
munication as natural as words between
them. They understood each other without
effort.

The cowboy wished it was half that easy
with women.

His sweetheart was an independent sort
with a mind of her own, and had little use
for him unless she was so inclined.

He needed to win the lady but wasn't
sure how to go about it.

Mick laughed quietly and sat back, his feet
propped up. That seemed all too appropriate to his current situation. He'd won his
way into Raine's bed, but he wasn't sure
about her heart.

That dark-haired beauty didn't want his
help, hadn't asked for it, and was as
dangerous as a loaded pistol ready to go
off. Part of him admired her feisty spirit,
but a bigger part wished she'd agree to
lean on him just a little more. Maybe his
days as a drifter were coming to an end,
because he wasn't going anywhere. This
valley felt like home and whether she
admitted it or not, she needed someone
like him around.

There was a reason for the price on his

head in Arkansas. He was damned handy with a gun. A man needed to be able to defend himself, and others if it came right down to it. Maybe someday he'd even tell her that story. But now there was trouble coming. He could smell it in the air and hear it in the whisper of the aspen leaves.

Could he write in a voice like Brighton's, one that was all the more powerful for its simplicity? Mick wasn't sure, but he *was* sure he was interested to find out what trouble was coming and how it worked out with the dark-haired beauty and the cowboy. What was the danger?

He was taking mental notes.

So he read on.

"We need more details."

Hadleigh Galloway, Melody Hogan and Bex Calder all stared her down. They'd known each other since childhood, and the tight-knit threesome were the first people Raine had thought of when she'd come up with the idea of the scholarship. All successful businesswomen and mothers, they'd done what she hoped and, despite their busy schedules, embraced the idea. Bex's wealthy in-laws had handed over a large sum of money as well.

It was no longer just one scholarship, they'd decided over appetizers and then an array of salads varying from shrimp to garlic chicken. They could now safely give out five from the current endowment. They had their usual table at Bad Billy's and the place was hopping due to the influx of skiers. The old jukebox was getting a definite workout, with an emphasis on Patsy Cline and Willie Nelson.

"Details?" Raine tried to look like she didn't understand the demand. "Of what?"

"Nice try," Hadleigh said after a sip of iced tea. "Let's talk you and Mick Branson. Don't ask how we know, because of course we do."

Drake was probably to blame, since he played poker with Tripp Galloway and Spence Hogan once a week, and he regularly bought horses from Tate Calder, so all their husbands were probably a font of information.

"I'm not sure what you want to know. He's . . . nice." Raine took another shrimp and popped it in her mouth to avoid the conversation. Billy's poppyseed dressing was so good it should probably be illegal.

Melody wasn't letting her off the hook. "In the looks department, I agree. Better than nice. Let's upgrade it to deliciously handsome. And there's no doubt he's successful. He seems to be spending a lot of time here in Bliss County all of a sudden. He spent Christmas Eve at your house and I'm guessing there was mistletoe involved. What's up?"

"He just came so he could see Slater's movie with the family as a surprise Christmas gift."

"I watched it, of course. It was fabulous. But nope." Bex shook her head. "A phone call at the right moment could have done the trick. Speculation has it he came here to see *you.* I have it on good authority."

"Whose?"

"Blythe's, via my mother-in-law. The networking around here is incredible."

Lettie Arbuckle-Calder *was* connected. "Like I don't know that," Raine muttered.

"I'd say he's not your type, but maybe I'm wrong." Melody, a jewelry artist, spoke thoughtfully. "I've met him and he has a soulful aura."

Hadleigh snorted. "You should have been a hippie, you know that? A soulful aura?"

Melody wasn't one to take anything from Hadleigh without arguing, even if they were fast friends. "Hippie, huh? Let's talk about someone who makes quilts for a living. There's hippie for you. I think you're the only person I know with an incense burner."

"That's an air freshener."

Bex said mildly to Raine under her breath, "I'll put a stop to this. Been doing it for years now. Otherwise it could go on for an hour." Loudly, she interrupted, "I think we were talking about Mick Branson, right? Tell us about him."

Too bad putting a stop to the bickering meant shining the spotlight back on Raine. "He's creative and imaginative, once you see beneath that corporate businessman image. Yes, he raises money for Slater's films, but that's because he sees the vision."

"Or the money." That was Bex, so practical.

"Nope. To see his face when the documentary came on at prime time on a day that isn't easy to secure was priceless. Mick did it for all of us. I'd say he moved heaven and earth to make it happen."

"You're in love with him." Hadleigh looked delighted. "I can see it."

"You can't see love," Raine argued, sidestepping an actual answer. She'd only just begun to admit her feelings to herself and to Mick. She wasn't quite ready to share them with others yet, not even friends.

"Yes, she can," Melody disagreed, jumping right into Hadleigh camp. "She has a special magic."

"She can. She's a wizard." Bex pointed a finger at her friend. "She's got a potion or something she takes."

"I do not," Hadleigh protested despite her grin. "There's no simmering pot, no incantations."

"Wizard." They said it accusingly in unison.

"I'm empathic and gifted with insight," she corrected loftily, then turned to Raine. "Do we have wedding plans yet?"

"No!"

"We will soon," the wizard decreed. "The resort will be perfect as a venue. Elegant enough for out-of-town guests, but convenient for everyone else. Blythe wouldn't dream of anyone else doing the bridal shower but her."

"He hasn't asked me." Raine had to point it out.

"What would you say?" That was Bex.

"It doesn't matter, he won't ask. If he wanted to get married, he would have by now."

The three of them looked at each other, and then burst out laughing. Melody was the one who said, "Honey, take it from three married women, it doesn't work that way. They only cave when they find the right woman."

"And once they do, they're pretty wonderful," Hadleigh informed her in a theatrical whisper. "Don't tell Tripp I said that because I'll deny it. Those cocky pilot types are full enough of themselves already."

"I agree." Bex's husband had also been a pilot before he decided to become a horse breeder. "And they're wonderful, only if given some instruction," she explained with a cheeky smile. "They need guidance."

Raine needed to rein in all this speculation. "Mick's well beyond the time in his life when he's going to ask without careful consideration, and he certainly would not ask *me*. I come with a daughter, a giant cat and a big blundering dog. Most of the time I live in faded jeans that are genuinely faded from being washed like a million times, and a handful of T-shirts. I decided when I was about twenty that high heels were overrated and haven't looked back. Besides, I live here and he lives somewhere very different. I will never be glamourous and I don't apologize for it, but he could get glamourous if he wanted it."

"Do you think that's the type of woman he wants?" Hadleigh considered her carefully. "It doesn't seem to me it is. He could have had that at any time. He's dated actresses, debutantes, and if I remember correctly, a very famous professional female athlete."

Raine weighed her words. "He's fallen in love with Wyoming."

"Or you."

Bex added, "Or both."

She wasn't convinced yet, despite his earlier declaration. "Maybe. I could be a passing fad, like when we were in high school and decided blue mascara was the way to go. That didn't last too long."

He'd said it though. *I'm falling in love with you.*

Her artistic bent seemed to fascinate him, and his desire to write did the same for her. Mick Branson had layers, and she needed that. He wasn't just Mr. Boardroom, he was also polite and thoughtful. That he'd wanted to make dinner for both her and Daisy was a winning strategy, that was for sure. He'd earned some definite points there.

She added, "He did fix me dinner."

All three of her companions glanced at each other and said in unison, "We know."

Of course they did.

Melody commented, "He's a goner. Ask the wizard."

"Goner," Hadleigh confirmed sagely, and Raine smiled, shook her head and gave up.

11

Mick read the entire manuscript in one day. Other than an extremely quick lunch with Raine that had ended with a brief and unsatisfying goodbye peck on the cheek because she was in a hurry and they were in a public place, he'd spent the rest of the time reading in his room. Dinner was room service, eaten almost absently as he read.

It was an indulgence for him and the unfinished work was fantastic.

No pressure.

It brought him back to his childhood when he'd read those first Matthew Brighton books. Being reminded of his father was welcome when he was now committed to changing his life.

Loyalty. Fidelity. Integrity.

He'd absorbed those lessons without need of a lecture. He'd bet most people thought his parents were frivolous due to their wealth, but they absolutely were not. His father had been demonstratively diligent as a family man, and as a businessman. Both he and Ran had learned a lot from him. Their father wasn't successful because it came naturally, it was because he worked at it, and his example had stuck.

Don't ever screw someone over and think that's okay.

They didn't.

When it goes south, regroup and think about how to fix it. It might seem like the end of the world, but it isn't.

Deal with hard guidelines but make them fair. No one loses that way.

Take time every single day to make sure you appreciate what you have. Ambition is fine, but avarice is not.

Raine was 100 percent on that one. It was clear she liked her life. Mick liked his, too, but recognized that the missing elements had nothing to do with money and everything to do with taking more time to simply enjoy himself. He didn't like busy airports and congested freeways yet had to put up with both on an almost daily basis and both of his houses were nice by any standard and luxurious by most, but a waste since he didn't use even half the space.

It was time to just sell them and move on. He realized now he'd been thinking about it for some time, even before his keen interest in this part of Wyoming had arisen. Maybe ever since he'd picked up his first Matthew Brighton novel and sat down to read.

His father would no doubt approve.

The last paragraph of the manuscript was: *He was a man of action and it wasn't in his nature to sit idly by and just let things happen. They happened on his terms and that was that.*

Mick dealt with talented people on a constant basis. That was his job, to win sponsors, to create backing for plays and films like the ones Slater did so well, to decide what was innovative and new, and what wasn't going to go over with a large viewing audience.

Now the tables had turned and he was the one sitting there on the creative edge . . .

Tentatively he opened a document on his computer and began to type. He was daunted, yes, but it was out of the question to not at least give it a try. Two hours later he had some words down and wasn't displeased with the result — not that he was impressed with himself, but it had come far easier than he imagined.

He sent Raine an email. Mission Aspen Trail conclusion has begun.

It was now after midnight, and of course

she typed right back immediately. You've been busy.

How was the meeting?

It was good. We're all pleased with the number of applicants. The scholarship is evolving into more than we imagined. There are a lot of good students out there who deserve the chance to make their dreams come true.

A very Raine sort of sentiment. The woman who preferred to give away an expensive piece of property.

Good cause, he typed back. I'll help, of course. You should get my mother involved.

Had he really just said that, in writing, no less?

Instantly he recanted. He loved his mother but she had a tendency to take charge and definite ideas on how things should be done. *Or maybe not. She might take over.*

We were talking about how we need someone to maybe run a foundation. Do you think she would?

Oh, I think you'd maybe raise a monster from the depths, but if you want meticulous management, she's your woman. That was honest.

Monster or not, she could be just what we need.

I can obviously get you in touch with her. Can we have dinner tomorrow?

We can but I have something else in mind. Call me in the morning.

Like?

Just call. And sweet dreams.

She didn't write anything further.

If he knew Raine she'd gone right back to work. He did the same, not returning to the manuscript but instead answering emails and checking his messages since he'd basically taken the day off. No news, no stock market updates, none of his usual routine, just moonlight on the snow and a sense of personal well-being.

He had no illusions that this was all going to be simple. Making a major change never was an easy process, but if he trusted his instincts at all, he had to accept that it was time.

■ ■ ■ ■

Occasionally she got some pretty hare-brained ideas.

Raine had to admit this could be one of them. She strapped the toboggan to the top of her SUV and Daisy clapped, her eyes shining. She was going to be taller than her mother, Raine had already figured out, taking more after Slater in that regard, and had that coltish lack of grace that would change as she matured. In any case, she was young enough to still think sledding was big fun, and maybe Raine was too, since she agreed. Samson seemed just as excited, romping through the snow.

Some kids never grew up.

Some grown-ups — namely her — just wanted to see Mick Branson rocket down a wicked hill on a toboggan. She could probably sell pictures of that. She knew the steep hill, and since she doubted he had a proper coat for this experience, had asked Slater if she could borrow one. They were very close to the same build. Of course the answer had been an amused yes once she explained why she was asking. He even said he'd love to film it, but his crew was all off on Christmas break.

"That's what my phone is for," she'd assured him. She could catch a short video of the urbane Mr. Branson careening down the slope if he had the fortitude to accept the challenge.

She somehow thought he would. So far he'd proven to be unshakable, even in the face of the entire Carson family, Jangles and his sneak attacks, talking to her grandmother, whipping up a dinner extraordinaire . . .

She'd see if those nerves of steel held up.

Red called it Dead Man's Hill and it was certainly a wild ride. He was the first person to point her in that direction with the admonishment it was not for the faint of heart. He was right. But the snow was perfect and it wouldn't be winter if she didn't at least go down that hill once a week, and Daisy loved it. Mick could decline if he wanted, but she had a feeling he would be game.

Raine doubted anything tripped him up, but she had to admit she was eager to see the look on his face when he first saw that slope. If a person didn't have a moment of doubt, then they just weren't sensible. What they decided after they stared down that 45 degree angle and thought it was maybe a bad decision but looked like it might be really fun, well, that was up to them.

Red had wisely counseled that if you didn't panic like a sheep that had eaten loco weed then you would be fine. Raine was uncertain how a sheep that had ingested that plant did act, but it sounded like solid advice to just enjoy the experience.

Mick pulled up, right on time as usual, and got out of his fancy rental, eyeing the contraptions strapped to the top of her car. "You've been out sledding?"

"No. Not yet."

"I'm beginning to see the light. This is why you told me to wear jeans."

"Yep," she responded cheerfully. "Hop in. I have the right kind of coat for you and Mace offered up a spare pair of snow boots since some hiking is involved. The good news for you is you get to carry the big toboggan. Don't worry, I have a thermos of hot cocoa."

"It had better have some whiskey in it," he said darkly, but gamely climbed in the passenger side on the car.

She jumped in and started the vehicle. "Has Mr. Boardroom ever been sledding?"

"Maybe when I was about thirty years younger. Are you sure my feeble body can take this?" He buckled his seat belt.

She eyed his muscular frame and broad

shoulders with true appreciation. "I think you'll survive."

"I guess I have no choice but to find out. I'm being . . . what's the expression out here in the wilds? Railroaded?"

"That's the one." She pulled out onto the street, which was clearing nicely after being plowed. The abundant sunshine helped, too, even though the temps were still below freezing.

Samson woofed from his spot next to Daisy in the back seat. "We're bringing the *dog*?"

"He loves it. I think he can ride down the slopes with you. At the bottom you get a special bonus since he always licks your face in exuberant gratitude."

"That takes dogsledding to an interesting level." He looked resigned. "This just gets better all the time. I was thinking a fire and maybe a glass of wine."

"We'll get to that. I'm making homemade pizza, by the way."

"That sounds fabulous." Mick scooted his seat back a few inches, careful not to jar Samson, who was curled up on the seat behind him. "Let me guess — smoked salmon and caviar on crème fraîche."

"This isn't Beverly Hills, hotshot. How about sausage, pepperoni, onion and green pepper."

"Or sardines, Gouda and watermelon." His tone was so serious she heard Daisy draw in a disbelieving breath from the back seat. "It's my favorite."

"Be careful," she said as she turned onto main street. "Or I'll get Stephano to fix that just for you."

"You guys are joking, right?" Daisy asked suspiciously from behind them. "Sardines are fish. That doesn't go with watermelon. And I've never had watermelon on pizza. It sounds gross."

"We're definitely joking." Mick gave a mock shudder. "I tried sardines once in college. I still have nightmares about it. Cans of sardines are following me around on tiptoe, begging me to give them a second chance."

"You're funny," Daisy informed him with the giggle Raine never got enough of hearing.

He did have a good sense of humor once a person caught on to the droll delivery. Raine was happy about that. Raine was . . . *happy,* she realized. Before he'd come breezing back into town she'd been very content. After all, she had a wonderful daughter, friends, a satisfying career . . . but this was different. She had to tamp down the hope that maybe Hadleigh the Wizard was right, and try to stay practical.

Even with the property and cabin he wouldn't be around much because he was a busy man. For that matter, she was pretty busy, too. So did their lives collide in the right way?

They might.

Let's see how he handles Dead Man's Hill.

"We're getting close." She headed for the road opposite the ski slopes. "You might want to try on the boots."

He toed off the loafers and picked up the boots she'd left on the floor on the passenger side. "I take it this will be an Olympic event of some kind. Call it a hunch."

"Depends on the snow. There's fast snow and slow snow."

"You'll have to teach me the difference."

"One will cause a sardine-like experience and the other is just fun."

"More nightmares?"

"Only if it's the fast snow."

He sent her a keen glare. "You're deliberately trying to scare me, aren't you?"

"Shoot, you found me out. Let's see if you're up for it."

The drive was scenic by any standards, and right there it was an especially high bar. The curvy road wound up toward the mountains and was crowded by trees, and for most people that alone was harrowing. Luckily she'd driven it enough times to know just when to slow down and take it easy. Some kindly good-old boy had plowed one lane with the blade on his truck and she hoped they wouldn't meet a car coming the other direction, but otherwise the climb was breathtaking. They parked at a scenic outlook the state had put there years ago, and turned to Mick. "Here's the hard part. It's easy to walk to the hill, but we have to hike back up towing the toboggans."

"It seems to me you've done this before, so we can certainly handle it together. I don't really see a hill though."

She sent him a mischievous grin. "You will."

12

The woman was trying to kill him.

That wasn't a hill. That was a champion alpine slope. Mick pointed at the bottom. "There's a stream down there."

Raine was blasé about that observation, looking absurdly attractive in earmuffs and a scarf. "You're going so fast and with the angle you sail over it, that's part of the fun."

"Uh, I think I weigh a little more than you do."

"No problem. I've seen Drake, Slater and Mace float right over it. Just brace yourself."

"Is this some kind of Grand Teton test?" He hefted the biggest toboggan off the roof.

She flashed a mischievous grin. "Trial by fire."

"I'm going to trust you."

"I think we've already trusted each other quite a bit."

She certainly had a point there. They had. She'd slept in his arms and he wanted a repeat performance in the worst way.

Daisy had bounced out of the car and was impatiently waiting. Samson seemed equally trusting this wasn't a suicide mission and was gamboling in the snow, so Mick had no choice but to take it on faith as well.

That was one hell of a steep mini-mountain. It looked neck-break worthy. "People have survived this?" he asked dubiously.

"You're looking at some of them right here."

"How many dead bodies buried at the bottom of Dead Man's Hill?"

"Hard to say. Headstones are covered with snow. You gonna chicken out?"

"Never." He wasn't about to give up that kind of dare. "Promise me a night together if we both survive?"

"Deal." Her hazel eyes held a teasing light. "I'll risk anything for that."

"Then hop on for the ride of your life."

"I thought we were just negotiating for that to come later."

She gave him the look he probably deserved for that comment. Daisy had already gotten on the smaller sled with the ease of someone who had definitely done it before. Samson had climbed on behind her and was furiously wagging his tail, a canine grin on his face, and she gave a whoop and pushed off.

"She's going to lord it over us if they win. Hurry."

Raine sat her very shapely behind down on the bigger toboggan and waved him on. Mick had to admit that despite having scuba dived off the Great Coral Reef and canoed on the Amazon, this had to be up in the top ten of adventurous things he'd done in his lifetime. He gamely got on behind her, wrapped his arms around her slim waist and said a small prayer she knew what she was doing.

The snow was deep enough they had a smooth trip, but they picked up speed at a blood-racing rate and he was pretty sure he didn't need the parka she'd provided because he broke out in a sweat. Their sled was heavier with two adults so they caught up with Daisy and passed her, Raine giving her daughter a cheery wave, and when the slope flattened out, they finally came to a halt in a swoosh of snow and triumph.

Daisy arrived about two seconds later, spinning around in a circle as she too came to a halt, breathless but laughing. "Hey, that's not fair. You had ballast."

Mick wasn't sure if he was more surprised she knew the word and could use it, or if he was insulted. "Big word for a small fry. And you had a little ballast yourself."

His mistake was to point at the dog. Samson took it as an invitation to come leap all over him, his enormous snowy paws dancing with such enthusiasm Mick actually staggered backwards.

Raine didn't quite succeed in hiding her merriment with her mitten clamped over her mouth.

Daisy was as saucy as her mother. "I may be a small fry, but at least I know how to handle a big dog."

He burst out laughing, trying unsuccessfully to fend off the dog's burst of affection. "You have a point there. Too bad he didn't help you win the sledding race."

"We'll see what happens next. Have fun carrying that big toboggan up that hill, Mr. Branson. Come on, Samson."

It *was* imposingly steep. "We have to walk up that? Maybe I should have ridden up on Samson."

"Great cardio workout," Raine replied without apology, handing him the rope to the toboggan. "Think about your heart."

"I have been lately." He gave her a meaningful look.

"Don't do that." Her gaze softened. "I'm already afraid I'm in too deep."

"Why be afraid?" It was hard to believe he was standing knee-deep in snow having this conversation.

"You don't even live close."

"I'm considering selling both my houses and moving here. I have a cabin apparently. I'm going to build a house. Remember, you're going to help me design it. I'll even buy myself a parka. Talk about *in deep.*"

"A parka? That *is* deep."

"Almost like a promise ring with weather-proof lining."

"Those are the best kind. That way you don't get cold fingers."

"I thought it was cold feet."

"What are we discussing?"

"You tell me."

"Branson," she said, starting to trudge up the hill — and it took some trudging; he definitely had his work cut out for him carting up that sled, "your love of talking in circles has to go. I'm sure that works well in Hollywood, but in these parts we prefer a more direct approach."

"You want direct? I'll give you direct. We might be too old for promise rings, but not for a more committed relationship. I'd like you to start thinking it over."

He wasn't quite what Red would call a straight-shooter. The kind of man who

179

slapped down his glass on the counter and asked for more red-eye, straight up.

He was tailored slacks, a linen shirt and a persuasive voice.

Well, he had on jeans at the moment, but he looked great in them. His dark hair was every which way, thanks to Samson, and he hauled up the toboggan without missing a breath, so he clearly had more facets to him than just boardroom suaveness. If she had to label his style, she'd call it tousled elegance.

He was also the creative, sensitive man who would finish an old Western novel.

Trouble on the horizon.

She thought maybe he'd just proposed. Or suggested it anyway.

The wizard was perhaps spot-on.

Raine pointed out softly, "We've slept together once."

"It was more than just sex, at least to me."

She was instantly out of breath and it had nothing to do with the steep slope of the hill. "To me as well, but —"

"I'm bringing to the table that I have some social and historical connection to this area. I like your daughter, I even like your beastly dog and that lion of a cat."

"This isn't a business meeting," she said, laughing. "Mick, we're walking up a nearly perpendicular hill in knee-deep snow. You really don't have to sell yourself at this moment."

"Hey, I'll have you know just coming down Mount Everest was a demonstration of my affection for your comely person."

"Comely?" Her brows shot up.

"I've been reading some old-fashioned Westerns lately. They use *comely*. That's a word that needs to be brought back. I'm just the man to do it. Consider yourself comely, ma'am."

"You might want to work on your Western drawl, cowboy."

"I can't fire a six-shooter, either. Never touched a cow in my life, and oddly enough I don't have the desire to herd one anywhere. I think you'd better go back to Mr. Boardroom."

It was quite the hill to climb, so her laugh was just an expulsion of frosty breath. "Please tell me you can ride a horse."

"That I've done. In several countries, including Argentina. And in Patagonia those vaqueros are a critical bunch."

"Where haven't you traveled?" she asked curiously as they soldiered up the incline. "Somehow I think that's a shorter list than the opposite question."

Blithely, he said, "I've skipped Siberia and

Antarctica. Too cold, though Mustang Creek in winter might just give them a run for their money." He sent her a wink. "I'm joking, but in reality, my parents dragged me all around the world. As I got older, I had to travel for business, so I ended up pretty much everywhere at one time or the other."

That was so different from Raine's conservative upbringing of childhood church camp and the occasional spring break vacation when she was in college. He came from money and she certainly didn't. Her parents were just hardworking middle-class people who weighed their finances based on what they could afford and what they couldn't, were practical and dependable and always there for her. What more could she ask for?

"We really couldn't be more different."

"So?"

"Would it work with you here?"

"My business schedule? Not all the time."

At least he told the truth. "I can't ask you to make that commitment."

"I think I'm asking *you.*" He plowed through a deep pile of snow. "I've never asked anyone before, so maybe I mean it."

"Maybe?"

"That was ill-phrased. I meant, you should consider maybe I really mean it."

"Do I seem hesitant?"

"Do I?" He tugged the sled over a big rock. "Glad we didn't slam into that on our way down."

"I knew it was there." Raine only wished she could avoid emotional pitfalls so easily. "No, you don't seem hesitant. That might scare me the most."

"On the same page then?"

"We could be."

She felt her heart warm despite the fact that there was snow in her boots and her toes were cold. Was it possible she'd just gotten engaged?

No.

Well, maybe. After all, the man *had* slid down Dead Man's Hill because he trusted her. He was going to *move* to Wyoming.

"Oh, I say 'maybe' and get in trouble, but you can say 'could'?"

This wasn't best time for verbal sparring because she was getting out of breath. Deep snow was great for sledding, but it was hell on wheels trying to walk through, especially up an incline like this one. Five seconds to get down and twenty minutes to climb back up. "We'll debate that over the glass of wine by the fire, okay?"

"I think we just came to an agreement on something."

"Can we agree on resting at the top of the hill for at least a few minutes before we attempt to become professional daredevils again? I felt like I was fleeing the bad guys in an action movie."

"Would we have escaped?"

"Oh, definitely. No one would be stupid enough to follow us down this hill, not even bad guys. At least we didn't crash into any of the headstones."

"Like the rock, I know where those are, too, but I admit with ballast it is a little harder to steer."

He laughed and hauled the toboggan the last length of the climb. "Maybe I should sit this next trip out then."

"Not on your life, Mr. Boardroom."

13

Warm, comfortable and there was no harrowing hill right in front of him. True, a very large and still-wet dog sat at his feet, not to mention the giant cat beneath the tree, but he'd started the fire while Raine made her pizza dough, and he had a glass of merlot in his hand.

When he'd gotten back to the resort, he'd even managed to write a few pages, including the ending paragraph to a chapter: *Her adventurous spirit never failed to captivate him, and the fascination didn't end there. She was comely, but he'd met other beautiful women. She was intrepid.*

If going down that slope at warp speed wasn't intrepid, he didn't know what was. He felt somewhat intrepid himself, so Raine definitely qualified.

He was starting to wonder if Matthew Brighton hadn't modeled this last novel's heroine after his lovely granddaughter.

It sure seemed like it.

Was Mick the hero?

A tall, dark-haired greenhorn was the main male character. He was starting to wonder. He didn't really believe in premonitions but he was changing his mind. These days, he couldn't help but feel that something was going on and he might be a part of it.

And he got to write his own ending.

Raine came in from the kitchen. "I didn't have watermelon. Or Gouda or sardines. I'm afraid you're stuck with my original recipe."

"I suppose I can live without sardines just this once."

"Harry makes the pizza sauce from scratch. Just wait. She could bottle it and retire. We all just hope she never will."

He couldn't see the always-bustling Harry ever content with retirement. "Was she ever married?"

Raine settled in next to him on the couch. "Harry? I think so. She's like Red. You can't ask too much. I skirt around those subjects like they're a rattlesnake ready to strike."

"Interesting analogy. Maybe you should be the one writing the rest of this book."

"I'll stick to graphic design, thanks. But my philosophy has always been that if something is private and a person doesn't want to talk about it, then they shouldn't have to. Life's too short. Don't stir the pot if there's no need." She planted her bare feet on the coffee table and wiggled her toes. She'd changed into plaid pajama pants and a faded shirt with a picture of Goofy on the front. "The fire is nice."

"After practically flinging myself off a cliff three times, I agree. I felt like I was competing in the luge at the Olympic Games."

Raine elbowed him. "Admit it, you had fun."

He slipped his arm around her shoulders. "As long as Samson enjoyed himself, that's what matters most."

"He did. Jangles is jealous. Look at him, all out of sorts."

"No offense, but he always looks all out of sorts." A pair of unwinking amber eyes was watching them stealthily through the branches of the Christmas tree. "I think he's spying on us."

"Probably wondering if we're going to make out on the couch, just like a suspicious father. That isn't a bad idea by the way. Daisy's not going to venture out from her room until her movie is done playing."

He'd never heard a better idea in his life. "I don't know if I have the strength after walking up that hill three times, but I'm willing to give it a try."

Raine's mouth curved. "I somehow think you'll manage."

He wanted one hell of a lot more than a kiss — or two — but would take what he could get. A beautiful woman in his arms and a crackling fire was his true idea of holiday cheer, and Raine kissed him back with her usual audacity, her fingers trailing along the back of his neck with tantalizing slowness.

If Daisy hadn't been in residence, and Jangles watching their every move, he might have at least tried to slip off her shirt and caress what he knew to be very lovely breasts, but he settled for just pulling her closer so he could feel them against his chest.

Naturally Samson decided to join them then, bounding onto the couch with great enthusiasm, not exactly adding to the romance of the moment, and both he and Raine were the recipients of kisses of the doggie variety.

So much for the romantic mood.

"It's a zoo here." She laughingly pushed Samson away to prevent another attack of affection. "I warned you."

"There are worse things than to be loved."

He picked up the dog — no small feat — and set him on the floor. That animal weighed about a ton and it wasn't done growing. Samson was a fitting name.

"I couldn't agree more." Neither could Samson, who decided to join them again. Mick gently but firmly set him back on the ground, avoiding another slobbering sign that the puppy stood behind him one hundred percent. "Don't get too flattered," Raine warned him wryly. "He loves everyone. Now if Drake's dogs love you, you're part of a special club."

"I want to be a part of a different club entirely," he told her quietly. "The 'If Raine Loves You' club."

She met his gaze squarely. "Aside from Daisy, I'm starting to think you could be the founding member."

"What about Slater?"

She considered the glass in her hand. "I'll always care about him. But we were more in lust than in love. When he offered to marry me it was just because he's a good old-fashioned nice guy. We'd already mutually gone our separate ways when I discovered I was pregnant. Luckily for both of us, I'm not an old-fashioned girl. You've seen how happy he is with Grace."

He had, and he wouldn't mind that for

himself at all. He thought about Grace and Luce and the serene glow that currently seemed to surround them both. He'd always thought that was a myth, but had changed his mind. Their happiness came through loud and clear.

"I want children." Those were his cards, right on the table. A straight flush, no request for more of the deck. He was afraid to be so blunt, but she deserved to know it. Besides, she had encouraged him to be more direct out on the hill.

Raine didn't bat an eye. "Slater and I . . . we were really young when I had Daisy. I've been thinking about it more closely now than I did then. I'm past thirty. I might not *get* pregnant. Can you live with that?"

"Of course." He squeezed her hand. "Life is a gamble. But one thing that's certain is how I feel about you. I risked Dead Man's Hill just to gain your admiration. I bought a purse to win over your daughter. When a grown man is willing to buy a cute purse, you know he's serious."

With a straight face, she agreed. "We'll put the purse in as exhibit A."

"Exhibit B might be making out on a couch like a teenager. That isn't boardroom behavior. You might be a bad influence."

Raine's eyes sparkled. "Just wait. Now, tell

me about the book. Gramps was working on it when he passed away, so I haven't been able to bring myself to read it. I'm not going to ask if it's good, because I know it must be. What's the storyline?"

She was admittedly curious.

Mick sounded very neutral. "A Tenderfoot imagines he's a cowboy and falls in love with a dark-haired independent woman and is determined to win her heart. There's some conflict with a neighboring rancher who wants her land. Sound familiar?"

How was it she'd imagined something exactly like that? Tears stung her eyes. "I miss him. It would have been so nice if you could have met him."

"No one could agree more."

"He would have thought you were a fine man."

"I hope he would have been right."

She smiled through her tears. "I know he would."

"That might be the best compliment I've ever gotten." He lifted her hand and kissed it. "I might comment that you now smell vaguely of giant puppy, but I think I might too, so I'll let it go just this once."

Raine was conciliatory. "You might want to get used to that. I don't think Samson will improve as he gets older. Plus your dog will be added to the mix. What were you thinking about? Giant dog, or a small one? Medium breed? What's our plan?"

"I can't ask you —"

"You didn't. I offered." She raised a hand. "So what was that boyhood dream?"

"Collie."

"Done." He seemed like a collie sort of man. It fit. "Long hair, just my luck. I'll tell Blythe, who will tell Mrs. Lettie Arbuckle-Calder and you'll have a collie rescue pup in no time. That woman will scour the state for one. She's a wonder. And don't tell me how you can afford to buy one, because rescue it is."

Mildly, he said, "You can be on the bossy side at times. Just an observation."

He was right. "I'm really used to running my life all on my own, and also making most of the decisions concerning my daughter. If it's anything big, of course I ask Slater, but we don't have a custody agreement because we've never needed one. Ultimately it falls to me to make the day-to-day choices. I warn you, like your heroine, I'm used to being independent."

"If you weren't, I doubt I'd be so interested. Not only do I have my hands full running a company and my own life, no matter how *comely* she might be, I don't want someone who just wants me to take care of her."

Raine practically spit out her sip of wine laughing but managed to swallow in the nick of time. "*Comely,* again. You and that word."

He shrugged. "A man on a mission, I tell you. Soon teenagers will be using it, nudging each other in the football stands on Friday nights. *Dude, look at that comely girl over there. Check her out.*"

"If anyone can do it, I think you can."

"Thanks for the vote of confidence." He was looking gorgeous, and cowboy-like in his denim shirt and jeans. Except for the hair. He needed a hat to really mess it up, and a set of boots and a horse. She'd get Tate Calder to help her with that last one.

Wedding present?

What else to give the man who probably had everything? She couldn't top that beach house in Bermuda.

An old six-shooter?

She did know Bad Billy had a friend who dealt in antique guns. Maybe she'd see what he could negotiate for her. Billy knew everyone.

If Mick finished this book, he certainly deserved something like that . . . unique and special. Very Old West. Something to hang on the wall of his new house.

She thought he'd love it. Hat and boots aside, he'd really go for the six-shooter. Raine got up. "Let me check on my pizza dough."

"It will have risen about two millimeters, Raine." He captured her waist and pulled her back. "Stay here with me."

She traced the line of his nose with her fingertip. "You are entirely too dangerous."

"I'm entirely yours if you want me."

"Mick." Her voice was hushed.

"I'm right here."

"I know. Your hands are doing interesting things."

"Nice?"

"Too nice. Jangles is still watching us."

"I'm going to have to get used to him giving me the stink-eye, right?"

"You are taking some risks. I wish I could invite you to stay the night, but like I said, I can't. Daisy is certainly old enough to understand why you would. I need to talk to her before anything like that happens."

It was almost disappointing that he immediately let her go and settled back into a more relaxed pose with a sigh. "My intellect is telling me I agree one hundred percent, but another part of me has a different take on the situation. Maybe you shouldn't dress so provocatively."

"These pajama pants and the T-shirt really are a little over the top. I'll try to tone it down."

"See that you do if you want me to behave. Maybe you could shave your head or get a giant tattoo of an elf on your forehead. I'm not positive even that would turn me off, but it would be a good start."

Raine laughed. "You've got the holiday spirit, I see. The elf might look strange in July, so I think I'll skip that one, and I happen to like my hair right where it is."

"There lies the crux of the problem, so do I."

At that moment Jangles prowled stealthily out from beneath the tree — which really meant he lumbered out, because he definitely could not pull off a quiet approach — and launched himself onto the couch between them, but couldn't quite fit. Mick reached for his wineglass and scooted away enough to give the cat room to settle down. "I think he's decided to help us out with the self-control issue."

"He's a very wise feline." He was. He definitely liked Mick. She did, too. "So what's Slater's next project? I haven't asked him yet."

"Becoming a father for the third time

comes first, I think, but I've heard some musings about the Snake River. After this last film, he'll be able to choose just about anything, I'd guess. Backers will be lining up."

"I like the idea." Raine was sincere. "It's beautiful country there. He'll absolutely remind people we moved west gradually."

"And the setting will win the day."

"I think so. His films work that way."

"He does have an eye for beautiful things. I'm looking at one of them right now." He held her gaze.

It was a nicely done compliment. "Thank you, but I'm hardly beautiful."

"Maybe not in a traditional blonde bombshell sense, but you're striking, and your eyes are unforgettable. I know I couldn't stop thinking about you. Slater is a smart man, so I was surprised he ever gave you up, but I didn't really know the whole story."

"I'm glad I got to share it with you." She hadn't been able to get him out of her mind, either. "Now, if you can chop some onions and green peppers, we'll really be on the same page. Follow me."

He could and he did, and she liked the sight of him in her kitchen, the Hollywood executive with a knife in his hand, frowning over the cutting board in concentration.

It might be a different kind of board than he was used to, but she was starting to think he'd adjust to the change.

14

She bent over to dip water out of the river, her hair in a makeshift knot that had come half-loose, her skirt hiked up over a pair of the prettiest ankles he'd ever seen as she waded in.

He'd die for her.

It was a possibility. There was a small local war going on as the ranchers squabbled over their land and she was vulnerable, a woman alone with a child, a lovely widow doing her best to hold on to what she'd fought to build. He wasn't about to let her lose it all.

Maybe he wasn't a fast draw yet, even though he'd been practicing, but he was a fair rifle shot, he'd discovered, and he could put food on the table. She'd made venison stew the night before that was so tender it melted in his mouth, and despite her guarded stance, he could tell she was starting to trust him. He now had his bedroll on that old front porch.

He felt like he'd gained something special right there.

The war wasn't over, but a skirmish had been won.

Mick eyed his computer screen thoughtfully, read it over again, and decided it fit the voice well enough, but wondered if it was too sentimental.

Maybe not. Men were every bit as sensitive as women were, they just didn't express it in the same way. His father had refused to get rid of the old rocker in the corner of the living room because his grandmother had given it to him, despite his mother's objections to the impact on her otherwise perfectly furnished space. It did stick out like a sore thumb, but he'd stood firm.

Though she came off as highbrow most of the time, Mick had certainly noted his mother had left it there even after her husband had died. That antique rocker stayed put. Maybe she was more sentimental than he thought.

So maybe he'd leave the writing as it was for now. He liked it. If a man would sleep on a woman's front porch, he was really into her, and willing to protect her. Hopefully Matthew Brighton would agree.

Especially on a day like today. The wind had picked up, he could hear it whistling by the windows, and even the ski slopes were empty. It was getting later, or maybe just felt like it because the skies were so gray.

He was trying not to crowd Raine too much, but he slipped out his phone and thought about it and then touched the screen. She answered almost at once. "Hi. What do you need? I'm swamped."

He grinned at her tone. Even clearly distracted, she was appealing. "This might sound crazy, but what if I asked Stephano to make a few sandwiches and throw in whatever other genius side dishes he has and we took dinner to the cabin? Daisy could come, too, of course, but I need . . . I don't know, a sense of place. You said the woodstove still worked, right?"

"There's probably a zillion nests in the chimney, even though I had it cleaned, so the whole place could go up in a plume of smoke, but as far as I know, yes. Slater just picked Daisy up so she can't come along, but I'm up for it. I need a break. Tell Stephano I'd love some of that garlic artichoke dip he's so famous for. I'll come get you. What time?"

He glanced at his phone. "Is two hours too soon?"

"No, perfect."

"Great. I'll call when I'm on my way."

He then phoned down to the room service number and asked for Stephano himself if possible. Probably thanks to his association with the Carson family, it was. "Can you make me whatever you think is your best sandwich, the artichoke dip Raine apparently loves, and anything else you'd add to an alfresco dinner for two in an old cabin? I'm putting myself in your hands."

"You have chosen wisely." Stephano sounded delighted as he announced, "I will wipe your socks off."

Mick almost mentioned that "knock your socks off" might be the more appropriate description, but he refrained. Stephano's English was sometimes as creative as his cooking. "I look forward to the meal."

"You should."

He hung up with an inward shake of the head and a grin. There was nothing wrong with self-confidence. Mick normally had a decent dose of it himself, but lately he couldn't count on it.

It didn't help that the front desk called and said a special delivery had arrived for him via special courier, and as he went down and signed the confirmation of delivery he knew that his life had just changed forever. Raine had turned down Slater flat. At the moment Mick was decently hopeful that that wouldn't happen to him. Although she'd pointed out how different they were, an observation he didn't disagree with, they'd then discussed marriage, even children and some future plans, so he took that as an encouraging sign. But he hadn't actually *asked* yet.

He'd implicitly trusted Ingrid to choose a stunning ring and he wasn't disappointed. Nestled in the satin lining inside the small box was a chocolate diamond exquisitely cut and anchored on a platinum band. The name of the jeweler making him lift his brows. The assumption she'd spent quite a chunk of his change on it was a given, but he planned on only doing this once in his life.

He felt Raine would love it. He sent off a quick text to his brother. Tell Ingrid I'm smiling. Thanks.

Ran texted right back. Good luck, loverboy.

He went back to his room, wondered what a man wore to propose at a haunted cabin at night, and finally decided maybe he should go shopping at some point because the best he could do was dark, tailored slacks and a white shirt along with his infamous loafers. Definitely vintage Mr.

Boardroom, but then again, he was living out of a suitcase at the moment. He hadn't known exactly what to expect from this visit to Mustang Creek.

More writing was out of the question. Instead he paced, tried to watch the news and turned it off since it was the wrong night to hear about what was awry in the world, and instead turned on a classical music station and checked his email. Not much going on during a holiday week and he was enjoying the respite from his normally hectic schedule, so that was just fine with him.

It was ridiculous, but he was nervous. Like he was seventeen and about to pick up his first prom date.

But he was far from seventeen, he reminded himself as he clicked off the computer screen. And he needed to get a grip. He took a calming breath, deep and slow.

He could handle this. Ask the question, hopefully get the right response, and if she chose to be as pigheaded as a feisty mule — a description he'd undoubtedly picked up from Red somewhere along the line — he'd reconsider his tactics.

The elegant bag with Stephano's latest masterpieces was delivered right on time and he was more than ready to make the call. "I'll be there in a few minutes with the requested dip in tow."

"I'll be ready."

I'll have the ring and the question.

He didn't say it, but he certainly thought it as he left the resort and got in his car. He did make one stop in town before he drove to her house, and when he pulled up the light was a warm, welcoming glow in her window.

He knocked and walked in when he heard her call out a welcome. Jangles of course went in for the kill, but by now Mick was ready for it and dodged away. Raine was smiling. "Nice move for a city boy. But he's going to mope. Give him a couple of treats to make him feel better while I grab my keys."

Of course, the cat understood every word. He followed Mick into the kitchen and stared unwaveringly at the correct jar on the counter.

Message received.

He got out a handful of treats and put them in the bowl. Jangles devoured them in about two seconds. Mick had an impulse to deal out more, but Raine came in then and said, "No, that's enough, he's playing you. He does that. Let's go."

She jiggled the keys.

He wasn't positive he was composed enough for this evening, but he decided to take his cues from Jangles, who had collapsed into a relaxed sprawl on the floor, his eyes half closing. His pose screamed: *stop worrying.*

Mick escorted Raine out the door. "Let's go while the food is still at least semi-hot. It smells like heaven."

"What is it?"

"No idea."

"You ordered it, right?"

He held her elbow as they made their way down the snowy sidewalk. "I gave Stephano carte blanche, though I did specifically request the dip you wanted. He promised I would be impressed — at least I think that's what he was saying."

"He does have a way with words, doesn't he?" She pushed a button to unlock the vehicle. "One of the many things I love about him."

He set the bag in the back and got in. "You don't mind driving in this weather?"

"No." She didn't, he could tell. "Wow, it does smell amazing in here."

"That man loves you right back. Whatever is in there is because I mentioned your name. I can take zero credit."

She backed up the car and they tackled

the street. "I'm already starving. The cabin, huh? I appreciate your enthusiasm but you should be forewarned this could be an interesting journey. The snow has somewhat melted off, but it's blowing around more than a little. Luckily this little buggy can handle just about anything." She patted the steering wheel. "I've been there a thousand times. I think I could find it blindfolded."

Maybe she'd been optimistic.

It wasn't whiteout conditions, but it was very near, and in broad daylight it was a challenge without a road of any kind, so in the dark it was close to impossible.

Mick seemed pretty determined that the cabin be their destination though, and she sensed it had something to do with the manuscript. She was pretty good at reading people and more in tune with him than most — and Mr. Cool, Calm and Collected was wound up about something. There was tension in his shoulders and a set to his jaw that said something was certainly on his mind.

Maybe it was just that he was making some big decisions, but she didn't think so. Mick Branson did that every single day and didn't even blink about it. He made up his mind and sailed on that ship full-steam ahead.

"There's a big drift by the porch," she noted out loud. "We'll be walking the last bit. Luckily there's still firewood piled inside. I brought a lighter for the lantern in case all the matches are damp and you should put on those boots Mace gave you."

"I bought some for myself, and a sleeping bag, some candles, and a fire log to get things going for our impromptu camping trip."

No wonder he'd loaded several bags besides the food into the back of her car. She'd wondered if they were going off to safari in deepest Africa.

Snow swirled around them in ghostly forms, circling the windows, brushing the hood, occasionally obscuring the entire structure. Raine put up her hood. "I'll go unlock that reluctant door if you'll bring the stuff in. I've got the food, so don't take too long, or it will all be gone. Just a friendly warning."

"Consider me warned. Stephano would never forgive me if I moved too slowly to sample his latest creations."

"The artichoke dip alone will make you weep with joy."

"I'm going to take your word for it, and

get inside as soon as possible."

The first blast of wind hit her square in the face. She'd watched the forecast and knew it was supposed to calm down, but it about knocked her over. She scrambled for the doorway, almost forgot the bad top step, and then struggled with the key.

The door opened like magic and she practically fell inside, first because she'd braced for its usual resistance and was caught off guard by its easy surrender, then because another gust propelled her from behind.

By some miracle Raine managed to keep her balance as she stumbled in, and despite the dark, she avoided the old couch that undoubtedly had mice in it and made it to the table. The lantern helped as soon she managed to get it lit, and just then Mick came through the door like a pack mule, loaded down with everything a man could carry and maybe more.

He panted, "I thought the wind was going to die down. I think it's getting worse."

She watched him dump the bags on the floor. "It is supposed to calm by dawn. I think we're spending the night right here."

"Well then, let's get the fire started."

Her grandfather never would have dreamed of using anything as modern as a fire log to light that old woodstove, but then again, it was remarkably handy. Mick knelt there, dusted in snow, and the log caught with one touch of a match. She was happy to see it seemed to be venting properly because the room didn't instantly fill with smoke.

"I brought a tablecloth from home. For all I know there's a bear hibernating in the single closet where things like that are kept, and I'm not going to look. Clean utensils and paper plates as well, since everything gets so dusty when it isn't used."

Mick agreed. "Let's not go bear hunting."

He was a typical man and had brought candles, but nothing to put them on, so she dug out a couple of old plates, and set the table and it was . . . well, nice. Tablecloth, candlelight and an undeniably attractive man. What more could a girl want?

Food, for one, and maybe some heat. Fortunately, the stove was starting to take care of the temperature, and the howl of the wind outside did add to the cozy ambience.

She was even able to take off her coat as they sat down to discover what wonders Stephano had prepared for them. One sandwich consisted of watercress and smoked salmon with aioli on French bread, the other one roast beef layered with what had to be artisan cheese and served in some sort of homemade rye that had flecks of fennel, too. There was also a pasta salad with tiny shrimp and Kalamata olives, not to mention Raine's prized artichoke dip, and to top it all off, a key lime cheesecake.

It looked delicious.

Quite the alfresco picnic. It was hardly a wild guess that food like this had never been eaten in the cabin before. "I suspect my grandfather subsisted on pemmican or something similar," she told Mick jokingly. "He did like good whiskey and believe it or not, applesauce. There are several groves of apple trees on the property. I remember the smell of applesauce simmering on the stove from my childhood."

"That stove has to be from the Civil War era. I've never seen anything like it."

"It isn't new, that I can promise you. But it works just fine."

"I can tell, since it is warming up in here."

The candlelight played nicely off the masculine lines of his face. If she hadn't seen him interact with Daisy and Ryder, holding babies, laughing with Blythe and Harry, and joking with the Carson brothers, she might worry more that she was influenced by his good looks. Being her, she blurted out what she was thinking. "Don't get all full of yourself, but you're as handsome as this dip is delicious."

Amusement lit his eyes. "Now there's a rare compliment. Because you made a really good call on the dip."

"I always make good calls." She shamelessly took another helping. "But lucky for you, there's plenty. Even I can't eat all of this. Stephano must like you."

"I'm starting to believe that. Just try the pasta salad. I want that at our wedding."

She was still mid-bite when he slid a small box across the tiny table. His smile was wry. "I would be on bended knee, but have a feeling that part isn't as important to you as the question itself. I would love it if you would agree to marry me, Raine. You'd have the last vote on the pasta salad being served at the reception, of course. The dip is a given."

"Yes." She didn't even hesitate, which spoke volumes to her.

And to him, which was reflected in his expression.

"You're sure."

"I didn't sound sure just now? What about you?"

"Absolutely. Now that's settled, maybe you'd like to open that." He nodded toward the box.

211

She complied and took in a deep breath. The ring was both gorgeous and unusual, and in the candlelight the gem in the exquisite setting winked with tones of brown and bronze. It was Mick Branson–style over the top, and she had no idea what to say.

"Mick."

He reached over. "I take it you like it. I think I'm supposed to put it on your finger, but I've never done this before. If I mess it up, let me know."

He definitely didn't mess it up.

He must have slid the ring on the right finger and said the right words because he was engaged.

Officially.

"Wedding date . . . when do you have in mind? Just wondering since I'm one hundred percent certain my mother will ask that question."

For the first time since he'd proposed, Raine looked uncertain. "I haven't even met her."

"Oh, she'll consider that an unimportant detail. She'll be so thrilled I'm finally getting married that she'll get immediately involved. I, for one, would like something very understated. But it's your day. I'll just be tagging along."

"Not so. You've promised to bring the dip.

212

You'll be the star. As for the date, I'd like mid-May. It's so gorgeous here at that time of year."

"Done. Stephano can cater. Perfect. That's settled."

"I loved Bex Calder's wedding dress. I might count it as my borrowed item, if she doesn't mind. We're about the same size."

"Food, dress, ring, date. Our work is done. As for my wardrobe, I'll wear pants, I promise. No one will be looking at me anyway, not with you in the room. My brother as best man, Slater, and Ryder as groomsmen and I think we have a wedding all planned. Let's keep it simple."

"You do remember you're Mick Branson, right?" She laughed and shook her head. "I somehow think it won't be simple. I believe celebrities will be invited and Ryder would be the most nervous groomsman on the face of the planet, and Drake would bring his dogs. My bridesmaids would all be pregnant —"

"So how about we set the date for sooner, with just me and you instead? I'm good with that." He was more than good with it. He'd marry her standing in a muddy field in a rainstorm. "Apply for a marriage license at the Bliss County courthouse and have it over and done?"

It was what he wanted. Simple. The fanfare held no appeal. If she wanted the big event — then of course, yes, every bride was entitled to that — but if he was given a choice . . .

He'd keep it low-key.

Raine put the last scoop of dip on his plate. "How offended would your family be? No movie stars, no corporate executives except you, not even them."

That he could assuage her on. "You do realize that being Mick Branson really isn't my agenda."

"You know, I do. I *love* that about you."

"There will be a party." He confessed that tidbit almost reluctantly. "My mother will want to throw a reception at some point, but quite frankly, everyone in my family travels so much that getting them all together at the same time probably means planning the wedding out a year or so, and I don't want to do that. I have zero desire to wait."

"If you think Blythe and Harry won't throw a shindig, you're dreaming, cowboy. So we're looking at two parties, and I doubt they'll be quite the same. I'll have to buy heels for one, and will be able to wear my favorite pair of comfortable old flats to the other. They could do that in May instead."

"We could just not tell anyone and let them believe we're living in sin."

"If you think Daisy wouldn't spill the beans, then think again, and I would tell her the truth." She took a bite of her sandwich and after she swallowed, said, "Oh my gosh, Stephano must *really* like you. We might have to set the cheesecake out on the front porch to save it for breakfast."

Raine would do that. She'd eat key lime cheesecake for breakfast without a thought.

She'd accepted his proposal in a run-down cabin in Wyoming during what he expected was now a whiteout snowstorm. The entire structure shook with the next gust of wind.

But unlike in the book he was writing, Mick mused with a private grin, he was not going to have his bedroll on the front porch this particular night.

15

He wanted to marry her.

She wasn't every man's ideal of a perfect bride. She had a child, a past, and her unconventional approach to life was hardly traditional.

But he had no doubt he loved her and that was all that mattered.

She'd said yes.

He didn't ask her the traditional way but while they were eating dinner. He didn't mean to quite blurt it out like that, but his emotions got the best of him.

It was every girl's dream.

A beautiful ring, a romantic proposal and killer artichoke dip.

Not to mention a wind velocity that measured off the charts. It was amazing that she couldn't envision a more perfect evening. If the roof stayed on she'd be amazed at the workmanship of those long-ago craftsmen that nailed it on.

While there was the probability of a rodent drive-by, and Raine wasn't unaware of it because they'd heard rustling all evening, the room was nice and toasty, and when Mick rolled out the sleeping bag and started to undress her, she was willing.

Extremely willing.

He shucked off his clothes just as quickly, joined her under the warm folds of the sleeping bag and kissed her softly. Not passionately, but with a gentleness that melted her heart. He said, "I've waited for you. I don't think I knew what I was waiting for. Now I understand."

She'd waited for him, too. "Right there with you. A man with good hair in a haunted cabin is a rare find. You're so warm. Hold me closer and protect me from the possible rodent population."

"I'm your knight on a white steed. No mouse will bother you on my watch."

He was a very aroused knight. She wasn't at all averse to that, either. "I'm petrified, but with you to save me from fearsome rodents . . . say no more."

"No problem there. And warm? I'm alone with you, so call it what it is. I'm on fire. Can we stop talking and do something else entirely? I want to make love to you and I suspect your car will be blown away at any minute and the cabin will fall down around us and I won't care."

No condom. She didn't ask for one and he didn't use one. They'd had that conversation. He was . . . perfect. Insistently passionate but not less than thoughtful and understood her every response to each touch and whisper, and afterward the wind keening outside was almost as sexy as the way her leg sprawled over his thigh when it was said and done.

Raine rested her head on his damp chest. "I do love you."

"I hope so, since we're engaged."

"That part doesn't matter to me as much as that I *love* you. I can't believe it."

"Can't believe it? I'm trying to decide if I should be insulted or not. You sound uncertain."

"About my feelings, not about you." She gave him a playful slap on the shoulder. "Give me some latitude. This hasn't happened to me before."

"Never found the right man? I, for one, am pretty glad of it. You waited for me." His fingers sifted through her hair. "I'm going to christen you my best Christmas gift ever."

"I intend to be."

"Good, because you succeeded."

"How are you going to finish the book? The last I read, our hero was sleeping on the front porch in a raging snow storm."

"I think he moves inside. She would never leave him out there in the cold."

"Of course not. I bet he likes it better inside."

"They hook up."

"I think you need to put it more eloquently than that." She nestled closer, knowing he would take her words for the teasing they were. Mick would never be crude.

"Easier said than done, especially for a rugged, solitary cowboy like him. He likes the fact that he found her — he likes it a lot. He just isn't too good at saying it."

"She needs him to say it."

She heard him take in a breath. "I'm guessing you're talking about us. I honestly think the moment I met you I knew I was falling pretty hard."

"I was talking about the book, Mick. I would never play you like that. You made a distinct impression as well, I might add. As far as I can tell, everyone in the entire Carson camp immediately cottoned on to how we were feeling. I don't think we should play poker with them until we work on our technique. Now, back to the book. How does it end?"

"I'm not going to tell you, because I don't really know yet. You'll have to read it yourself when it's finally done. I don't know if my writing is on a par with your grandfather's, but I'm really enjoying it. It's coming more naturally than I might have guessed, probably because I've read pretty much all his books. He's so descriptive. Maybe that's why I have such a connection with this part of the country. I'd been here in my imagination often enough before my first visit."

"Well, this cabin certainly qualifies as the real deal. I'm surprised there isn't a musket mounted on the wall somewhere. On a night like tonight I'm surprised there *are* still walls."

It was wicked out there. She was warm and cozy enough in the afterglow, but the weather wasn't very friendly. Raine was glad Daisy was safe and sound at the ranch. If she had to call it, she suspected they might be stranded for longer than anticipated — the drift by the front door wasn't getting any smaller. "We could have a hard time leaving in the morning."

"Fine. I'd stay like this forever."

That was as good as *I love you.*

"This is a nice sleeping bag."

He chuckled. "I forgot pillows. I didn't think of it. I don't camp too often."

"I'll use you as my pillow. You're actually quite comfortable."

"That type of high praise is likely to win my heart."

"I had that in the bag already, right?"

"I thought that went without saying."

Raine rolled on top of him, which was very easy to do since they were sharing a single sleeping bag. She said simply, "I'm happy."

"That's what we're supposed to do for each other."

"I hope I'm holding up my end of the bargain."

"You have no idea."

She touched his lower lip, their mouths just inches apart. "Oh, I think I have some idea. Otherwise I'm guessing you wouldn't be quite so enthusiastic about one small sleeping bag with two bodies and no pillows."

"I thought I was your pillow." He held her closely, lightly stroking her back, those long fingers taking some definite liberties.

"And you're a good one. If you could market you, the stores would sell out. Women would flock in."

"Unfortunately, I think I'm taken, correct?"

"You got that right, mister."

Hands down, it was the most erotic night of his life.

In bed — well, technically in a sleeping bag — with a very sexy woman, and she'd fallen asleep all draped across him, not that she had much choice because there was nowhere else to go. It gave him some time to reflect on his recent life decisions.

If he sold both his other houses he could build her the house of any woman's dreams, but he didn't think she'd go for it. Raine would probably prefer something modest, but a dream artist's studio was a definite must. Maybe after Daisy graduated high school Raine would be willing to move to the cabin property full-time.

His wife. He was starting to get a real charge out of the notion.

Water, electricity, internet, a decent road . . . He could arrange all of that.

He had an idea forming in his head about the floor plan. As long as Raine basically agreed with it, he was in a very good place. She was focused on details and he was focused on what would work. A one-time-only construction project was his goal and he thought it was hers, too.

He liked pairing the right backer with the right film, and the right artist with the right project, because he could spot solid worth. He'd probably shot himself in the foot by even proposing that Raine consider doing the pixel film. She would be busier than ever, but *he* was ready to slow down and take a look around. His frenetic working pace couldn't go on forever, he'd always known that. If he cut back, he could be there a lot more of the time for Raine and Daisy — and any kids he and Raine might have together.

It seemed to him they'd started working on that tonight.

Those select casual relationships he'd had in the past amounted to nothing and he knew why now. He'd known something was missing, but just not how to define it.

Raine had settled all that.

And now he knew how the book ended.

"I did something wrong." He knew he had. She was quiet, and maybe not distant, but certainly distracted.

"No," she told him in a resigned voice, "you did something too right, I'm afraid."

How was that possible? he argued in his mind, but the spitfire was good at calling his hand. "The land dispute is settled. That varmit won't ever threaten you or this place again. What now?"

She put her hands on her hips, but at least now there was laughter in her eyes. "*Varmit?* Eastern boy, you need to learn a great deal about how to say a word like that. You can't pull off cowboy just yet, but you're pretty good, I'll grant, at solving a real problem without just taking out a gun."

"A man can use his brain now and then instead of force. I still don't understand why you're mad at me."

"I'm not mad, just pretty sure I'm going to have a baby."

He'd known it was possible, but he was still stunned. "What?"

"That isn't necessarily all your fault, I was there too, but in case you haven't noticed, we aren't married."

He recovered after a moment. And he could solve that problem, too. "There's a preacher in Mustang Creek. Let me hitch up the horses. We can pay him a quiet visit and take care of that right away."

She was going to be stubborn to the last minute, but was so beautiful every time he looked at her she took his breath away. "The last time you did that it didn't work out so well. I seem to remember sitting in the buckboard and watching you jump out to chase the loose horses down."

"Sweetheart, I remember. Thanks for reminding me you were laughing so hard I thought you might fall off the seat."

"I'm not sure I should marry a green-horn."

He went over and kissed her. "I'm positive you should."

Her smile was predictably saucy. "I think I will. I'll hitch up the horses."

EPILOGUE

December 24th, one year later
Was this a mistake?

Maybe it was — it was going to be hard to tell until it all settled out, but still Raine had fingers and toes crossed.

It was official, she was nuts for even thinking of this, but then again, Stephano and Harry had done most of the work. In a rare truce, they'd coordinated the menu and though they hadn't necessarily cooperated with each other, they'd grudgingly come to an agreement on what to serve.

The new house was complete, if not quite ready for guests since she'd been more than a little busy, but Hadleigh, Melody and Bex had put up decorations and Grace, Luce and Kelly were on kid patrol.

Mick had mentioned he was looking forward to green chili cheeseburgers and an old Western movie.

Not this year. His entire family had agreed

to come.

Was she nervous? Oh yes. Not because she was worried the party wouldn't go smoothly, but because she wasn't sure how her surprise was going to be received. Mick seemed to accept just fine that his family didn't spend Christmas together, but she wanted to give him this special gift.

A really wonderful gift hopefully, with a small bonus.

She'd talked it over with Blythe and gotten full Carson approval on the idea. So he had no idea his family was coming, and everyone was forbidden to tell him.

The new house did look wonderful with all the decorations. The tree was from the north end of the property and at least twelve feet high, but a ladder and three Carson men squabbling over who was ascending it took care of the top part and Daisy and Ryder had fun decorating the rest. Ryder was getting to the age where that sort of thing was no longer his idea of fun . . . He'd rather be taking cute girls to the movies, and — she wasn't a fool — maybe thinking about stealing a beer or two here or there by his age, but he obligingly hung up a snowman on a branch that Daisy wasn't tall enough to reach, asking if it was where she wanted it. She imperiously made him move it over three inches.

He really was the nicest kid and humored Daisy without protest.

The Bransons were the first to arrive. Raine had met them on a swift trip to California that combined personal affairs with business, since she also met with the director of the pixel movie. Mick's mother was cool and poised, but still warmer than expected. Not haughty, just assessing. His brother was very businesslike but equally likeable, and his sister-in-law was unexpectedly a kindred spirit with her keen eye for art. They'd met for dinner at some trendy restaurant so conversation hadn't been very personal, but Raine had started exchanging emails with Mick's mother, which he found quite amusing. She'd sent pictures of the house construction, of the sun rising over the mountains, of Mustang Creek's fall festival, of Mick and Daisy absorbed in a game of chess, all designed to give her mother-in-law a glimpse into their lives.

To her surprise, it worked. She got back not just replies, but photos of vineyards, theater signs, and even a Halloween photo of Mick's mother dressed up as Scarlett from *Gone with the Wind* for a fancy party. They might be many miles apart but they were finding a way to get to know each other.

Raine was convinced that while Mick shrugged it off as if his family never spending Christmas together since his father died didn't bother him, it did. She was hardly a psychologist, but she had to wonder if it didn't bother all of them and scattering to different locations was a way to avoid the emotional impact.

Time to start better memories, or so she hoped.

When Mick walked in the door, looking wiped out after a trip to Germany that took three days longer than planned, he was greeted by the sight of a houseful of people having cocktails and nibbling on artichoke dip. He stood for a minute in the doorway before he said calmly, "I saw the cars, so I guess I'm not surprised at the crowd. Raine, I talked to you last night. You failed to mention we were having a party."

She kissed him. "Surprise! It was really your mother's idea. Welcome home."

He kissed her back, taking his time about it. "My mother wanted me to have a party? Now I have two women conspiring against me — three, if we include Daisy. I feel outnumbered."

"Well, maybe we'll have a boy to help tilt

the odds. I'm due in July."

"What?" He looked like he might fall over. "Can you repeat that? We're having a baby?"

"It seems like we are. We've been trying, remember? Don't look quite so incredulous."

"*I've* certainly have been doing my best." He scanned the room and froze. "Is that my *brother* pouring himself a drink? He's here? On Christmas Eve? In Wyoming?"

"Don't look now, but your mother is right there in the corner, talking to Blythe and Ingrid. I have no idea what they're saying but I'm going to bet you're the main topic of conversation."

"That's a bet I'd be crazy to take. And nice job trying to change the subject. Raine, really? We're pregnant?"

"I'm pregnant and you're the father, so the answer to that is yes."

"I'm . . . I don't even know what to say. Why didn't you tell me?"

"It seemed like the perfect present to surprise you with. Last year you got a haunted cabin. How is a girl going to top that one? It was a high bar."

"I think you just cleared it." He reached for her again, but laughing, she pushed him away.

"Tonight you can tell your family face-to-face. Let's go celebrate. Mace made a non-alcoholic wine drink just for me, called Bran-Son. Drake has a new foal about to drop he's going to call Brandy. You know those two. The race is on, boy or girl."

"My family isn't up for this crowd. Or for Mustang Creek. This isn't Paris or Rome."

"No." Raine hooked her arm through his, her eyes shining. "It sure isn't. But I think they'll find they prefer it here."

He certainly did.

ABOUT THE AUTHOR

The daughter of a town marshal, **Linda Lael Miller** is the author of more than 100 historical and contemporary novels. Now living in Spokane, Washington, the "First Lady of the West" hit a career high when all three of her 2011 Creed Cowboy books debuted at #1 on the *New York Times* list. In 2007, the Romance Writers of America presented her their Lifetime Achievement Award. She personally funds her Linda Lael Miller Scholarships for Women. Visit her at www.lindalaelmiller.com.